Tattoo

Karen Lee [...] adelphia and now lives in London, where she works as a development co-ordinator for the European Script Fund. *Tattoos and Motorcycles* is her first novel.

KAREN LEE STREET

Tattoos and Motorcycles

INDIGO

*In memory of Laura Busch,
a poet in all respects*

First published in Great Britain 1995
by Victor Gollancz

This Indigo edition published 1996
Indigo is an imprint of the Cassell Group
Wellington House, 125 Strand, London WC2R 0BB

© Karen Lee Street 1995

The right of Karen Lee Street to be identified as author
of this work has been asserted by her in accordance with
the Copyright, Designs and Patents Act, 1988.

A catalogue record for this book is
available from the British Library.

ISBN 0 575 40026 9

Printed and bound in Great Britain by
Guernsey Press Co. Ltd,
Guernsey, Channel Isles

96 97 98 99   10 9 8 7 6 5 4 3 2 1

Contents

III. *Lost in Space*

I speak only for those who leaped and fell, losers being the only ones with something to say and no one to say it.
– Nelson Algren

I

Big Dreams

I

Big Dreams

It seems to me that here, the age, the weariness, and the sorrow of the old world has been left behind. That this is a breaking out in a new place, or rather that this country and people, and we ourselves, are a new creation, fresh from the hand of God, and with a new promise!

We have no royal road to distinction in our country. We have no ready-made great men ... If any would be great, he must achieve greatness. Nearly all of our heroes and statesmen have struggled up from the humblest places.

    – Emma Dorothy Eliza Nevitte Southworth, from her novel *India: The Pearl of Pearl River*, 1856

I say that you ought to get rich, and it is your duty to get rich ... The men who get rich may be the most honest men you find in the community. Let me say here clearly ... ninety-eight out of one hundred of the rich men of America are honest. That is why they are rich. That is why they are trusted with money.

    – Russell Conwell, from his lecture *Acres of Diamonds*

Actually, only a small minority of the human race will ever consider primeval nature a basic source of happiness ... Mankind as a whole is too numerous for its problem of happiness to be solved by the simple expedient of paradise.

    – Robert Marshall, an early explorer of the Brooks Mountain Range in Alaska

Within the Confines of Maps

Tinicum grew and spread with startling speed. It could be compared to a sudden infestation of poison ivy. Or a tumour, seemingly inconsequential, but malignant by intent.

No architect's hand had traced the boundaries of the place. No compass or ruler had been employed. It had evolved at Darwinian pace, then spontaneously exploded with a big bang. It was still a very small dot on the map, but like a star within a solar system within a galaxy within the universe, it had its peculiar order in the vast scheme of things. And a particular sense of self-importance.

Yes, Tinicum started out small, but it was a model for something all-encompassing. It nurtured the promise of untold riches and vast fortunes. It was a place where dreams would come true and a person could get ahead in life. Expectations hovered silently, mere shadows keeping a ruthless sense of order.

Tinicum, Pennsylvania, USA was the epitome of the space age. And like a rocket ripping upwards through the stratosphere, beyond the confines of oxygen and gravity and into the delicate fabric of space itself, Tinicum would discover something finer and better. Tinicum would launch a whole new way of life, something impossible to resist.

Chocolate Hearts

Vince used to give Lucy a big heart-shaped box of chocolates every week but she never suspected anything was funny until she found the gun at the bottom of the bag of groceries.

Vince was a good-looking guy. Kind of mean, she had to admit, but when he drove through town with the convertible top down, all the girls would turn and look. Lucy used to like that.

Lucy had met Vince while she was working at the Bunny Club in Willow Grove. He kept buying her drinks and drove her home the night she was fired. That was her friend Charlene's fault.

Lucy had only been working at the club for just over four weeks. She didn't like it very much, but needed the money. Eddie the manager let her mix drinks behind the bar instead of just waitressing. He liked the idea of a topless bartender and said he'd try Lucy out, but for less money than someone who had their certificate from bartending school. Clyde, the head bartender, didn't like it though. It upset the hierarchy between bar staff and waitresses. Lucy didn't think Clyde liked women much. He thought women with anything larger than a B cup were all boobs and no brains.

But Lucy stuck it out. She didn't think she had much choice really. She needed to make a living and didn't seem to have any skills beyond taking care of two kids, a house in the suburbs, and a motorcycle mechanic husband.

She still missed Rusty sometimes, but knew she didn't love him. She and Rusty had been divorced for almost two years, since June of 1967, after exactly seven years of marriage. She still thought about Rusty almost every single day. Sometimes she came across something from his tool kit, or a piece of some old motorcycle he had been working on. Or she would see someone with a particularly good tattoo and wonder if it was one Rusty had done. Every once in a while the smell of a freshly cut lawn or the taste of beer straight from the bottle made Lucy pause, waiting to hear the sound of Rusty's laugh. And every time she made hamburgers for dinner she would start chopping up raw onions without even thinking. She and the kids hated onions – the smell, the taste, everything about them. But Rusty used to pile them on top of his burgers. He'd grab Lucy, Franky and Katie in a big hug after dinner and would roar like a lion in their faces while they squealed and struggled against the power of 'the Almighty Onion'. Lucy would always throw those freshly cut onions straight into the garbage disposal, but her cheeks would be damp from their pungent insistence. Yeah, she still missed Rusty every now and then, but it wasn't love. She wasn't sure it ever had been.

Lucy felt relieved when she landed the job at the Bunny Club. The money Rusty sent her wasn't enough for them to live on and the bank account was hitting an all-time low. A feeling akin to panic had been stirring just beneath her rib cage. It was sink or swim time – every day she went through the Help Wanted section in the paper, but never found a job that she thought she would get. Lucy had never learned to type or take shorthand and had no experience in sales. All the jobs that sounded interesting seemed to involve something along those lines. Then Lucy started thinking about restaurant work. Waiting on people she thought she could do. She called about twenty places, but they all said that they were looking for experienced waitresses. 'I've been waiting on two kids and a husband for a quarter of my life – how much more experience than that do I need?' she finally shouted into the phone before it clicked into disconnection. Then she saw an ad for the Bunny Club:

Good Looking Gals needed for Exclusive Club.
Friendly atmosphere. Excellent pay. Call now!

OK, thought Lucy. What have I got to lose? She dialled.

'Yeah, come on in,' said the woman at the other end of the phone. 'And make it tonight. We're understaffed.' She gave Lucy the address and hung up.

It turned out that the voice had been Charlene, who had nothing to do with hiring or firing. But the manager seemed to like the look of Lucy, handed her a bunny outfit, and told Charlene to show her the ropes. So Lucy found herself dressed in approximately half a black leotard, fishnet tights, high-heels, and a fluffy white bunny tail and ears.

Charlene poured her a triple vodka with a dash of tonic and said, 'C'mon, kid, knock this back. It helps.' It didn't help quite enough and Lucy spilled a few drinks out of sheer nervousness. By her third night, Lucy's hands weren't shaking quite so much and she was less frightened that someone would recognize her or that her parents would somehow find out how she was making a living.

Lucy's parents definitely would not have approved. They didn't believe in divorce, so she hadn't dared to ask them for a loan when she and Rusty split up. Topless bar work was another story altogether. They probably would have disowned her – backed up by very vocal, long-distance comments from her sister Joycie. But Lucy didn't think there was much chance of running into her parents or any of their friends at the club. Only special customers were allowed in. If one of the guys from the neighbourhood did come in for a drink, he would never tell anyone he saw Lucy there. Being at the Bunny Club was kind of like cheating on your wife.

Lucy started working five nights a week straight off. Her best friend and neighbour June stayed with the kids until she could afford a babysitter. 'Don't worry about it, Lucy,' she said. 'I can watch TV, then have a little nap until you get back. It's not like Walter is going to have a tough time. Caroline will be in bed and he can always have the guys over to our place if there's a poker game on. It's not like Tinicum is a hubbub of activity on a Friday night or anything. Maybe we should come down to your club some time – once you get set up with a sitter.' Lucy couldn't quite bring herself to tell June that she was working in a topless club and that June and Walter might not have such a good time there. But she did think that June would probably understand if she ever did find out exactly what kind of place Lucy was working in.

The manager of the Bunny Club, Eddie, spent most of his time drinking with the regulars and encouraging them to buy another round. He was usually on the wobbly side halfway through the evening and would go take a nap in his office about midnight. Clyde thought it was his duty to make sure the place kept ticking over and, in particular, to keep the waitresses in line. He spent more time prowling around the club and snapping at the waitresses than mixing drinks.

'Get a move on it, you dumb Bunnies,' he growled. 'I know there's nothing between those ears, but get those tails twitching.' Then he would flick a waitress on the bottom with a wet bar towel, more than hard enough to sting and make her just about drop her tray of drinks.

It was hard to move around the Bunny Club at any great speed. It was a place designed to have a classy, space-age look. The bar was long and had twenty bar stools pulled up to its formica edge. Then there were a lot of little tables crammed close together on a level two steps down from the bar. These tables each had a candle and an ashtray on them and were supposed to give the place an elegant, intimate look. But really they just made it harder for the waitresses to negotiate their way past the big men who sat huddled over their drinks. Puddles of beer and sticky cocktails would often accumulate in the alleyways around the tables, making it easy for the waitresses to skid in their spike high-heels and go flying. 'Rule of the house,' Clyde would scream at them over and over. 'Don't spill the drinks on customers. Hold those trays high and steady. If you feel yourself going, aim for a customer's lap – but don't drop the drinks. Give 'em a cheap thrill, but don't spill. Got me?'

'Yeah, Clyde,' they would sigh each evening in resignation.

The dancefloor was a real danger spot at the club. There were two routes to and from the bar for a waitress: down the two steps and through the seating area, or across the dancefloor. Clyde liked the waitresses to work a circular route: take orders from those sitting at the tables, collect empties from the edge of the dancefloor and bring them to the bar, then take drinks back to the tables. The dancefloor was a small wooden floor drenched in sweeping coloured lights. A glitter ball sparkled above it. The effect was dizzying. Bodies moved in drunken disorder and elbows and feet were a terrifying obstacle course for the less aggressive waitress. This only added to Lucy's preference for working behind the bar.

It was the Saturday night of her fourth weekend at the Bunny Club when disaster struck. By this time Lucy knew all of the regulars by name and Vince was one of them. He had come into the club every night Lucy had worked and had sat at the bar while she mixed the drinks. Vince told Lucy jokes and crazy stories and made sure none of the other customers got too friendly. She was grateful for that and for the drinks he bought her. Lucy didn't feel so visible after knocking back a few doubles.

It was real busy that night – the Willow Grove bowling team had won the league cup and were celebrating hard. Susie called in sick and it wasn't easy to keep the customers happy. 'Out on the floor,' Clyde growled at Lucy. 'We need real bartenders working back here tonight. Go do what you were hired to do.'

Deborah, Charlene and Lucy ran around like crazy on their high-heels, but it was never fast enough. They'd set down one tray of drinks and someone else at the other side of the room would start waving at them. Charlene was getting into one of her moods and 'accidentally' spilled a Martini on one guy when he pulled her tail for the fifth time that night. Then a fat slob of a guy started snapping his fingers at Lucy and Charlene when they were both going past with trays full of drinks.

'Listen, Buster,' Charlene said real loud. 'It takes more than two fingers to make me come.' The thing Charlene didn't know was that the fat guy was Mickey Donnegan and Mickey Donnegan owned the Bunny Club. Clyde just smirked when Mickey complained to him.

'Just let me take care of this myself, sir,' he sneered. 'You,'

Clyde shouted at Charlene. 'And you,' he snapped, pointing at Lucy. 'You're fired.'

'Stuff your job,' Charlene said as she ripped her tail right off and threw it in his face. Lucy was proud of Charlene and they went out laughing, but she did wonder how she was going to pay for the groceries that week.

It was about midnight when they stepped out the front door into the parking lot. They were laughing and still wearing their ears. Charlene was doing an improvised bunny hop towards her car when this big red convertible pulled right up in front of them.

'You ladies need a ride?' It was Vince, revving the engine each time he dragged on his cigarette.

Charlene gave Lucy a wink and said, 'I'll just hop along home myself, sugar. Here's the number of the Cha Cha Club. I could probably get you a job there. The owner is kind of sweet on me. Call me there on Tuesday night. Bye!' Charlene wiggled over to her silver T-bird and zoomed off waving before Lucy had even climbed into Vince's convertible.

'Cigarette?' Vince tapped the pack once on the dashboard and one cigarette slipped neatly from the pack, almost into her fingers. He held the dashboard lighter in her direction.

'Thanks,' she said as casually as she could. Lucy felt different talking to Vince without the bar between them.

'So, you out of a job?' Vince asked.

'Looks like it,' she said. 'Clyde never liked us much anyway. At least Charlene went out in style.' She told Vince what she had said to Mickey Donnegan and he almost swallowed his cigarette he laughed so hard.

'Let's go get a pizza,' Vince suggested. 'I think this is something to celebrate.' They drove real fast to the Willow Grove Pizza Palace. 'Maybe you better wait here,' Vince said as he leapt out of the car. 'I kind of like the bunny ears, but the service might not be so quick with you dressed like that.' He grinned as Lucy went red and tried to stuff the ears into her handbag.

Lucy lived in a place called Tinicum which was about fifteen minutes away from Willow Grove, but Vince got them there in ten. Lucy was clutching the box with the large pepperoni and mushroom pizza as tight as she could and tried to keep a smile on her face that didn't slip into a look of terror. 'Nice neighbourhood,' Vince said as he zoomed the car around the block and then screeched into Lucy's driveway.

'Thanks.' There was a small break in her voice that she hoped Vince wouldn't notice. They got out of the car.

'Grass needs cutting,' Vince commented, taking a swipe at it with the edge of his foot.

'Guess so,' admitted Lucy. 'I'm usually a little too tired on the weekend to get around to it.' She looked at the grass which was peppered with dandelions and crabgrass. It was easy to see where her lawn stopped and Walter's and June's began. The bulb in the lamp at the end of the driveway was burned out and only the light seeping through her living-room curtains and the feeble glow of the quarter moon lit up her yard. It didn't look too good. It was the first time Lucy had really noticed. She wondered what the neighbours had been thinking. Katie's bike was lying on the grass, right next to her lawn ornament. As they walked past it, she gave the red metallic globe a quick polish with her elbow.

'Hey, what's that?' Vince laughed. 'A weird crystal ball or something?' He spread his hands above the globe and said in quavery voice, 'I can see a tall, dark man stepping into your life, young lady. A tall, dark, *handsome* man.' Vince cackled like a demented witch while Lucy tried to shush him. The front door creaked open and June stood there, a sleepy look of confusion on her face.

'Thought I heard voices,' she said. 'But they didn't fit in with the programme I was watching. I'm June.' She extended her hand to Vince.

'Vince.' He shook her hand vigorously. 'Real pleased to meet you.'

'Well, guess I'd better be going.' June arched her eyebrows at Lucy.

'Stay for some pizza if you want,' Lucy invited lamely. She pulled her coat tightly around her, more worried about June seeing her outfit than the cool April weather.

'Not hungry,' June replied. 'I'll call you tomorrow. See you again some time, Vince.' June smiled over her shoulder and winked at Lucy as she trudged next door.

'Nice neighbours,' Vince smiled. 'Ready to eat? Hope you have some beer – the stuff I've got in the trunk is a little warm.'

They walked inside. The place was a mess. Lucy started apologizing, but Vince walked straight into the living room, pushed a few of the kids' toys off the couch and plunked down in front of the television. 'I'll just get us some beers,' Lucy said.

Lucy opened the refrigerator door and let the cool air circulate around her face. She pulled out a six pack and put it on the counter next to the dishes from that night's dinner. Lucy half wondered whether or not to wash up before going back into the living room. She walked to the kitchen window which looked out over the backyard. She could see the Jamesons' house – someone was still awake. The rest of Tinicum was dark. Not many people in the neighbourhood had jobs that kept them up until after two in the morning. Lucy could see part of the street from her window. Cars gleamed under the weak glimmer of moon. Each house had a yard; a neat green square of equal measure. The houses looked pretty much the same – just the front doors were painted different colours. Only Lucy's house seemed different. A little worn out and rough around the edges. A little like Lucy felt.

She wondered what her neighbours really thought of her. She remembered the neighbourhood in Philadelphia where she had grown up. It wasn't good to be different there. She remembered when her grandfather had lived with them and how much her mother had hated it. Old Pops was a cantankerous man and no one understood him. Lucy thought he had liked it that way. Her grandfather wasn't too popular with the neighbours – or with her mother. No one seemed to like to have people living near them who didn't belong.

Yet nobody who lived in Tinicum really belonged there. Tinicum used to be farmland and was parcelled out into houses in the late 1950s. Young couples moved out of the city where they had grown up and created a place that wasn't quite like anything anyone had ever seen before. It was new. It was modern. It was ideal for raising a family and for young couples to make a better life for themselves. They were living in the space age and that meant endless opportunities. Nobody really belonged there, but the place was theirs. It held the promise of better things. It was a big dream that would come true for those who belonged.

Lucy was never sure that she had ever fitted in very well. June did – and June and Lucy had been best friends ever since she could remember. They came from the same place and the same kind of family. It wasn't Lucy's background that was the problem, but something within Lucy herself that wasn't quite right. When Rusty was still living there it hadn't seemed to matter whether or not they really fitted in. But now it was another story. A woman with two kids living on her own, bringing strange men home in the early hours of the morning. Jesus . . . Lucy pulled open a beer and took a long drink. She could feel Tinicum around her and wondered what it was thinking.

'Hey, the pizza's getting cold!' Vince's voice echoed from the other room. Lucy tried to hide her nervousness and walked into the living room with the beers. Vince was watching a horror film on TV and had made himself comfortable with his feet up on the coffee table. Lucy sat down and he put one arm around her shoulder and reached for a beer with the other.

Lucy wasn't too sure what they talked about that night, but they managed to get through a six pack of Budweiser before the pizza box was empty and another one after that. She had this feeling that a couple of times she called Vince 'Rusty', but she wasn't really very sure. Lucy kept sipping nervously from her bottle, sometimes trying to focus on Vince's face and other times happy to let its edges shift towards something more familiar. She vaguely remembered spilling her beer when Vince suddenly kissed her. She remembered nothing at all about how they got from the living room, up the stairs, and into her bed.

Next morning Katie burst through the bedroom door and jumped straight on the bed before Lucy was even awake. This was how Lucy usually woke up, but Vince didn't take too kindly to it.

'What the hell!' he half shouted while trying to pull the sheet up over him.

Lucy opened her eyes and the pale yellow walls moved up and down in front of her. She squeezed them shut again.

'Who are you?' Katie asked while jumping up and down on the bed like it was some kind of trampoline.

'Who are you?' Vince wasn't looking too happy.

25

'I'm Katie,' she said. 'I live here.' She stopped jumping and looked at Vince expectantly.

'Oh yeah,' he said and tried to smile. 'I forgot about you and your brother. Don't you believe in knocking or something? Don't you have any manners, kid?'

'I live here,' Katie said stubbornly.

'Morning, honey,' Lucy said real fast as she opened her eyes again. 'Why don't you go and pour some cereal for you and Franky. We need a little more sleep. Go watch the cartoons.'

Katie, hands on her hips, looked at Lucy for a minute, then shrugged her shoulders. 'All right. But don't forget you promised to take us bowling today.'

'Listen, sweetheart, it feels like someone is bowling inside Mommy's head right now. So why don't you go and quietly make breakfast for you and Franky.'

Katie jumped up and down a few more times. 'You promised,' she said.

'Please,' Lucy wheedled.

'All right.' Katie then bounced straight off the bed and almost into the hallway. Lucy held her breath and stared at the open door, waiting for Vince to say something.

'Jesus,' he said. 'Is it like this every morning? Don't you have them trained or something?'

'Kids have minds of their own,' she said. 'You teach them all you can and then kind of hope for the best.'

'You've got to keep them in line,' insisted Vince. 'A belt here and there keeps them in shape. You've got to make kids listen.'

Lucy didn't know what to say to that and changed the subject. 'What do you want for breakfast? I think we have Cornflakes or Sugarpops.' Lucy looked for her bathrobe as she spoke. She spotted it thrown across the chair, just out of reach from her side of the bed. 'And I guess you want some coffee,' she said nervously as she tried to slip out of bed with the covers half wrapped around her. She grabbed for the robe and put it on. 'Coffee?' she asked again, a little more calmly.

Vince gave Lucy a funny look then said, 'Yeah, coffee. And Sugarpops.' He propped the pillows against the wall, sat up in bed and lit a cigarette.

Lucy got used to having Vince around just like she had got used to working at the Bunny Club. It felt pretty uncomfortable at first, but after a while it all started to seem natural to Lucy: sleeping in the same bed with someone she didn't know very well and going to work at the Cha Cha Club three times a week while Vince sat at home drinking beer and watching TV. The Cha Cha Club wasn't bad – the waitresses were fully clothed and Lucy could concentrate on her bartending there. After a few weeks she had all the favourite cocktails and their prices down pat. Vince was OK with the kids. He didn't really pay much attention to them, but the notion of hitting them every once in a while seemed to have left his head.

At first, Katie and Franky weren't that impressed with Vince and kept out of his way. Then Franky decided Vince was OK, but Katie started calling him 'Stink-face'. Normally she said this behind Vince's back, but every once in a while she made a big production of almost saying it to his face. The kids both liked to hear Vince tell stories though. He'd tell them flamboyant tales about robbing banks and toting a gun. Lucy sometimes worried that the line between fact and fiction was a little blurry. The kids liked listening to Vince better than watching westerns on TV. He would spin them some yarn, then play shoot-out at high noon. He even bought Katie and Franky some cowboy outfits.

June thought Vince was great with the kids. 'He's a good

influence,' she said. 'Franky and Katie need a man around the house. So when's the big day?'

Lucy thought things were going pretty well too. Until a couple of weeks later when Katie and Franky were caught breaking into an empty house dressed like cowboys and armed with cap guns that had been strong enough to break the picture window. Vince was an influence, all right, but she was beginning to wonder exactly what kind of influence he was.

Otherwise, everything seemed OK and they were all living together pretty much like a family. Every Friday night they had this slap-up meal after Vince went to the supermarket and picked up the week's shopping. And every Friday Katie tried her best to drive Vince completely nuts. It was a point of honour with Katie and she rarely failed to win her special battle.

It normally started with Katie peering under the kitchen table and whispering, 'Here, Killer – come here, boy!' She would make kissing noises and snap her fingers.

'What's your kid doing?' Vince asked every time. 'What the hell is she doing?'

'Just feeding the dog,' Katie answered, throwing something from her plate on to the floor.

'Stop that!' Vince shouted. 'There's no dog down there.'

'Yes there is,' Katie argued. 'He's right there. Sniffing around your ankle ... ' Then she laughed and laughed, with her head underneath the tablecloth. 'Stop that, Killer!' she giggled now and then. Then she resurfaced and went back to her corn on the cob. At regular intervals she sneaked some food down to the dog and made whistling noises between her teeth.

'What's the matter with that kid?' Vince demanded. 'Can't you stop her from doing that?'

'Stop it, Katie,' Lucy said with resignation.

'Stop what?' Katie asked. 'I'm just feeding the dog.'

'There is no dog and you know it!' Vince shouted. 'Either your kid is seeing things or she's crazier than her father.'

'My father isn't crazy,' Katie retorted. 'He's smarter than you are. Bet you don't know how to make a tattoo.'

'Jesus,' Vince snarled.

'Don't, Killer!' Katie shrieked. 'Don't bite him! It's not nice.'

Vince had inadvertently jerked his leg back and hit his knee on the underside of the table. It happened every time. And every time Katie squealed with laughter.

'What is wrong with that kid?' Vince shouted. 'There's no dog and she knows it. What the hell does she think she's doing?'

'I'm just exercising my imagination,' Katie said smugly. 'At ballet class, Mrs Pepperidge always tells us to exercise our imagination and pretend we can dance. So I'm exercising my imagination and pretending we have a dog. It's obvious. Can Killer and I be excused please, Mommy?'

Later on Lucy would corner Katie and plead, 'Can't you just try and be nice to Vince?'

'I am nice,' Katie would retort. 'Anyway, I live here and he doesn't. He's only visiting. He should be nice to us.'

Overall, Lucy thought Vince was pretty nice to them. He mowed the lawn, he fixed a few things when they broke, he even went grocery shopping once a week. And after shopping, Vince always brought home a big heart-shaped box of chocolates for Lucy – the ones that sat in a beautiful row of red, purple and pink hearts with huge curled ribbons wrapped round them and a bunch of plastic orchids stuck on the front.

'Sweets for my sweet,' he'd say sliding the box of chocolates along the kitchen counter and into her hands. Lucy started to get kind of sick of the chocolates, but she hung each heart-shaped chocolate box lid on to the kitchen wall, and before she knew it there were sixteen boxes all lined up in a row.

Vince seemed to go to a different supermarket every week and never brought home a very consistent selection of groceries. Lucy would end up stopping by the local Acme a couple of times a week herself to pick up the basics like milk and cereal, kitchen towels and Comet cleanser. She didn't mind this as the local Acme was something else. Vince rarely went in there – he said it was too much to tackle.

The local Acme was managed by Bobby Silverelli. Bobby's ambitions lay well beyond being a supermarket manager. He was determined that one day he would be a famous rock and roll singer and more people than the shoppers at the Acme would know his name and hear his voice. Every Friday night, the Acme was open until 8 p.m. and Bobby would host a special performance. He would stand at the back of the supermarket, next to his twin brother Billy, and the two would perform the weekly specials. Billy played the organ and would accompany Bobby as he sang out their songs about canned tomatoes or frozen orange juice or sirloin steak on special.

The shoppers loved the Silverelli Brothers – they'd be moving down the aisles with their shopping carts, pulling stuff down from the shelves and slinging it into the carts in time to the music. They felt privileged to get a free musical performance while they shopped and felt it was their duty to support the local talent. Bobby Silverelli wasn't just a starstruck youngster – he was a pretty canny businessman as well. The takings on a Friday night soared when he and Billy did their act, and the Acme bigwigs were impressed with his initiative.

It was during one of these special performance evenings

when Vince decided to hit the Acme. Lucy wasn't there, but she heard all the garbled accounts later, about the same time the Silverelli Brothers sent Lucy a thank-you card after their launch into fame when they sang the whole story on the 'Ed Sullivan Show'. But that was weeks after the event, and the night Lucy found the gun at the bottom of the grocery bag, she was pretty confused.

She was standing there with the gun in her hand, just kind of staring at it when she heard Vince yelling, 'Lucy, where's that vodka I brought home? Time for a little more bartending practice!'

Lucy was just about at the end of her bartending course. She had seen an ad in the local paper for evening classes in 'the Art of Cocktail Mixing and Bartending'. It was only $49.95 for eight lessons and Lucy would be awarded a 'Genuine Bartenders' Certificate' if she passed the exam. Lucy was sure that a certificate would help her get a better job. Her teacher, François, used to be head bartender at a very classy restaurant in New York City. He would demonstrate how to make a few cocktails, then would give the students a list of drinks to practise making at home. During the final exam, each student would be asked to make twenty cocktails picked at random from the official bartending course book that François had written himself. Vince would help her practise most every night by drinking all the cocktails she was learning to make. He would pick a drink from her bartending book and she'd have three minutes to make it. Vince shouted from the living room again.

'Come on, Lucy! What's up? Don't keep the customers waiting!' She grabbed the bottle of vodka and hurried in to Vince, still feeling a little shaky just thinking of that gun in the kitchen. He was propped up at the bar Rusty had built in the corner of the living room. An assortment of alcohol

31

was on the counter top and Vince was studying her bartending book.

'OK,' Vince smiled. 'A Nutty Squirrel. Three minutes and go!' He stared at his watch while she dumped the ingredients in the blender and tried to calm down.

'There you go,' she smiled and handed Vince his drink. He downed it in a few gulps, then asked for a Fuzzy Navel. This went on for just over an hour; Vince picking different cocktails from the bartending book, Lucy mixing them up, him drinking them down. It was just about midnight and Vince was wobbly, but wasn't going to give up until he had drunk himself under the table. She was hoping that would happen soon because Vince got pretty mean during the stages between relaxed drinking and being under the table. She kept thinking of the gun in the grocery bag and a bad picture started piecing itself together in her head. All that shopping in all those different places during the last few months . . . what had been going on? She decided to give June a call and see if she knew anything.

'Where are you going?' shouted Vince.

'To give June a call.'

'No you're not. I need another drink.' Vince smashed a glass against the wall to emphasize his point, then threw another one which broke on the wall near Lucy's head. She ran up the stairs and grabbed her pocketbook, the car keys and a plastic raincoat which was the first thing she could find to cover up her pyjamas. She pulled the kids out of bed.

'Katie, Franky, let's go. We're going for a ride!'

'Where are we going?' Katie asked.

'We'll talk about it in the car. Let's go!' She picked up Franky and grabbed Katie's hand. 'Come on now, let's go.'

'But, Mommy, you're wearing your pyjamas,' Katie said, pulling up her own.

'I've got a coat. Now hurry up,' she answered as they ran

for the stairs just as Vince was crawling up them. Drunk wasn't the word for the state he was in. He was carrying something. Something about the same size as the gun. Lucy kicked the laundry basket at him and he went rolling down the stairs.

'Yay, Mommy, touchdown!' shouted Franky. They all ran down the stairs and out the front door. 'Bye, Vince,' Franky called.

'Bye, Vince,' Katie waved, then blew him a raspberry.

Lucy dragged the kids out the front door and towards the car. She pushed them inside and jumped in the driver's seat just as Vince managed to stumble out the front door. She got the car going and was starting to back out of the drive as he went for the driver-seat door. She slammed the lock down and accelerated in reverse. Vince jumped on the hood and started thumping on the windshield, madder than hell. Lucy hit the gas harder and he rolled off on to the driveway. She started driving as fast as she could towards the turnpike. Lucy knew she had to leave town for a while. Vince was mad and Vince had a gun and that was enough for Lucy.

'It's time for a vacation, kids,' she said, trying not to sound too nervous.

'Where are we going, Mommy?' Katie asked.

Vince had met all of Lucy's friends and family. It was no good staying with someone near to home. He would definitely find them. Particularly as it seemed clearer and clearer that Vince was an armed robber – small-time, maybe, but enough to get thrown in jail. And Lucy was the one person so far that could make sure he ended up there.

'Are we going somewhere fun for our vacation, Mommy? Somewhere we can go swimming and stuff?' Katie persisted.

Lucy thought for a minute. 'Yeah,' she said. 'We'll go somewhere fun. Somewhere with swimming.'

'Good. Then we can go and visit Daddy,' Katie concluded. 'He invited us last week and you said that maybe we would. You *said*,' Katie emphasized.

Somewhere like Florida was probably a good idea and Rusty wouldn't mind. Katie had a point. Rusty was the only person she knew that lived anywhere south of the Mason-Dixon Line. Lucy knew that she could count on Rusty. He was a pretty reliable guy. 'That's right, we're going to go and see your daddy.'

'Yeah, Daddy!' the kids shouted, then settled down and talked about all the fishing and swimming they were going to do in Florida, until they got bored and fell asleep for an hour.

'Hey, Mommy,' Franky said, the sleep still in his voice, 'I'm hungry. Are we almost there yet?'

'It's going to take a while, hon,' Lucy answered. 'You have to be patient.'

'Do you think old Stink-face will try and get us again?' Katie asked.

'I told you not to call him Stink-face . . . and, well, I hope not,' Lucy answered, feeling a stab of fear.

The kids curled together and fell back to sleep. Lucy's eyes continued to flick from the road to the view in the car mirror, then down to the kids in the back seat. The turnpike stretched endlessly in front of them, glowing faintly under the streetlights, punctuated by toll booths. Lucy wasn't sure exactly where they were heading for and where they would end up. It felt strange leaving Tinicum, and she wondered every now and again what their neighbours would think about the whole thing. Lucy kept on driving straight through the night, fear slicing up her stomach in hard, mean strokes. Her eyes never stopped searching the rear view mirror for any sign of a shiny red convertible moving in fast, like death, behind them.

Truckdrivers Used to Whistle at Her Mother

The Sunoco sign was the focal point of the town, which was little more than a gas station, a grocery shop, a post office, and a hotel-bar called the Elephant Inn. This town was called Tinicum, and Tinicum Pike was the only route in and out of the place. Eloise Hegarty used to sit on the front porch and watch that road for hours.

The population of Tinicum was twelve on a good day, six on a bad one. Grandma and Grandpa Hegarty, Eloise and her six-year-old daughter Greta lived at the Elephant Inn. It was a big stern-looking building made from wood and painted white. Its long windows had black shutters like eyelashes framing them. A porch extended from one side and offered some shade from the summer sun. The Elephant Inn was about five paces away from the grocery store. The Hegartys ran both of them.

Old Man McFarland and his wife had a tiny white house straight across Tinicum Pike. The house was attached directly to the post office and Old Man McFarland was the Postmaster General. His wife worked in the post office too, selling stamps and some novelty postcards.

The two families could sit on their porches and watch

each other. There wasn't a lot else to see in Tinicum – just the long dirt road that separated the two houses and miles and miles of cornfields that went on for ever. From a distance, Tinicum looked like three white ships lost against an endless swishing of dark green sea.

The Hegartys and the McFarlands were the official population of Tinicum. But sometimes truckdrivers arrived late with a hankering for a real bed. Or one of the farmers knocked back too much beer to find his way home. Then they would rent a room for the night at the Elephant Inn. Inn was kind of a strong word for it – it had a tiny bar and a few extra rooms upstairs which were rented out for a dollar a night. Everyone that stayed there was treated like family and could stay as long as they liked. Everyone thought it was a good idea to give the population a boost every once in a while.

Things went on pretty much the same from day to day in Tinicum, time more measured by the corn growing than the sun moving around the sky. Greta would get up real early every morning and run down the stairs, her cracked leather shoes tapping a loud staccato on the carefully polished wood. She would bang open the screen door, pelt across the front porch, and land in a heap on the grass. A sharp breath would explode in between the furrows of her ribs. Greta would press open her lids and turn around to look. And she would be there. Her mother was always there first, dressed up perfectly, looking wide awake. Greta would shade her eyes against the morning sun to see her mother better. The light bleached the colours of her dress slightly, but Greta could still see the perfect polish of her shoes and how the summer hat was perched so carefully on her mother's pale blonde hair. She would watch her on the swing, moving as gently as the leaves of corn that floated in the fields around them.

When the truckdrivers came, Eloise counted out the beer bottles from the fridge. She collected the change, then sat on the porch swing, moving back and forth in the breeze. Eloise never said much – just smiled while the beer was pouring and the change was clinking. She smiled while the truck doors slammed and the drivers whistled as they pulled out of town.

Tinicum was always the same. It was a special occasion when someone rented a room at the Elephant Inn. Then Grandpa would bring out his old fiddle and sit down on the front porch. He played long and loud to any old moon that was listening. It was strange how many of those drunken truckdrivers could sing. 'Just like Catholic choir boys singing,' Grandpa always said. 'Just like they're directing their thoughts straight up to Heaven.'

Many of them would sing about the bad times that were going on. The Great Depression they called it. They sang about never knowing what you were going to find when you woke up in the morning. About never knowing what you were going to have left. Or they sang about being on the road with nowhere to go like all those people they kept talking about on the radio. People piled into old trucks or maybe just set off walking, trying to find the right direction through the dust that moved in heavy swirls around them. They liked to sing what some people called the Blues. Maybe their past was busy resurrecting itself on those narrow, dusty roads connecting the Elephant Inn with the rest of the world.

Those evenings seemed the best thing in the world – music sailed every which way through the night and the fireflies decorated the dark even better than the stars. Eloise just sat on the porch swing, rocking back and forth, not even in time with the fiddle. She just smiled that smile and looked at Tinicum Pike. Her blonde hair shifted gently on the breeze. Her dress was always clean and fresh and her little high-heeled shoes always matched just right. Greta liked to look at her mother for a long long time. She was like someone in those movies they showed in the theatre down in Erwinna, but she didn't talk so much.

Early every morning Greta would run down the stairs, across the front porch and land in a heap on the grass. Fear would make her turn quickly. But her mother was always there first, in a different dress and looking wide awake.

The truckdrivers would come and the truckdrivers would go. Year after year. And they would drink and sing and whistle at Eloise. They would tell her stories about how good it was on the road. They would ask her to come for a ride.

Greta didn't like it. Truckdrivers whistled at her mother. Whispered in her ear as she dropped the change into their hands. Tried to touch her bright blonde hair. Every morning, Greta ran down those stairs and out on to the porch, fear cutting into her. But she would find her mother still there, drifting gently on that swing, smiling her smile, just watching Tinicum Pike.

Tattoos and Motorcycles

He clicked the radio on and pushed the volume way up. It was some kind of modern music, but he didn't care. He hated music anyway. He just wanted the noise.

Pops went to the windowsill and took down a small pot of red gloss paint. He selected a fine brush from a glass jar on the table near his bed. He set this carefully on some newspaper which covered the bedside table. With the penknife he carried in his shirt pocket, he prised the lid off the paint.

Pops looked carefully at the white plastic radio. There were a few scattered pencil lines across its surface. He understood exactly what each one meant. He took the eraser end of the pencil and stirred the red paint. He dipped the brush. Slowly the indistinct lines on the radio were covered with red as he moved the brush delicately over the radio's surface.

Pops surveyed the radio. Nearly done. The intricate patterns were something like the hex signs on barns in the countryside. Something like the fancy designs around the figurehead on a ship. Pops went over to the bureau and pulled out his bottle of dark rum from underneath the underwear. He shifted the hiding place several times a week so his daughter-in-law couldn't find it. He swigged it straight from the bottle. She always knew exactly how many glasses ought to have been in the kitchen.

Pops sat and thought a while. He hated that room. He hated that house. He wasn't too crazy about any of them either. Max was his son, the only one of his twelve kids that would put a roof over his head. Not that he should feel grateful for that. Max was only after his money. That's what a family's like. It will grab for every last cent you've got.

Pops sat on the edge of the bed for a good two hours. The bottle was empty longer than he realized. Yeah, he didn't like them much. The wife was too tidy and threw her weight around. Emma, his wife, had been too tidy – but Fred had always kept her in line. And the kids – two girls. At least there weren't twelve.

Twelve kids, for Chrissake. Emma had been bad luck from the day he met her, but he still couldn't figure it out. He was off on the ships for a couple of months at a time – hardly ever home. But when he came back for maybe a few weeks, Emma got herself pregnant every time. Twelve kids. He thought about the sea for a while. It made him mad, that small room painted white.

Pops stumbled down the flight of stairs and through the living room. The two girls stopped playing cards and looked at him. He went into the kitchen. He was hungry, but didn't know what he wanted. The refrigerator was big and white with one of those handles that pulled down like the arm of a slot machine. He pulled. There was a roast of beef in there waiting to be cooked. Pops wanted a steak or something, so he went to a drawer, pulled out a carving knife and slivered off some meat. He thought cooking it might be a good idea, but Pops wasn't in the mood. He took a small bite. Not much good. Pops lost his temper and took a swipe at the beef with his knife. He took a couple of the daughter-in-law's beers and lurched back upstairs.

The girls sneaked around the corner and peered into the kitchen. The refrigerator door was open, the carved up carcass dripped juice on to the linoleum. 'What do you think he was doing?' asked Lucy.

'Making dinner?' offered Joycie.

Pops slept for a little while, radio still playing loud. Lil came home from work and muttered to herself when she heard the noise. Damn him, she thought. Why couldn't Max have a normal father? Or at least a dead one?

Pops dreamt of the sea. It was 1885 and he was fifteen again, aboard his first whaling ship. He remembered the overwhelming smell and sound of the ocean, the first time he stood on deck and could see nothing but water surrounding their tiny ship. He had run away from his small village in Germany for what he thought would be a romantic life exploring the world.

His father Frederick Stitzenger had managed to get young Frederick an apprenticeship with the village sign painter Herr Moritz. But young Frederick hated Herr Moritz with a passion rare for a thirteen-year-old. Herr Moritz was a perfectionist with no imagination. He would beat Fred if he dared embellish the smooth lines of Moritz's style with fanciful designs or colours. After two years of what seemed to be endless beatings because of Fred's single-minded determination to defy Herr Moritz, Fred decided he was destined for a life at sea. He had walked past the harbour every day on his way to and from the workshop and had seen boys his age working on the ships. Fred imagined that their life would offer him a freedom he would never find in his small village. Fred talked his way on to a whaler run by a decent enough captain. He left without a word to his family or Herr Moritz and swore never to set foot in the village again.

Although life at sea was nothing like Fred had imagined, he liked everything about it. He learned to drink, how to play a winning game of cards, and started collecting tattoos straight off. First he had an eagle put on his right forearm; then a tiger running clear from just above his left wrist to his elbow; and then the panther on his upper back. Most of the tattoos he designed himself. He explained this to the women he picked up easily and frequently whenever the ship docked in a port. Years later, one drunken night in Philadelphia, he had 'Emma' tattooed on to his right biceps. He'd seen a lot of the world, but that last tattoo marked the end of his travels.

There was a rap on the front door, then Dot poked her head through and called out, 'Anybody home?'

'Hey there, Dot, come on in,' Lil said. 'You're just in time for a beer.'

Dot walked into the living room just as Lil came out of the kitchen, holding two bottles of beer. Lil handed one to Dot as they sat down in the armchairs. 'Thanks,' Dot said, and took a sip.

'How's tricks?' Lil asked.

'Oh, pretty good. Why is Lucy standing in the corner?'

Lil sighed. 'Same old story. She's being punished for being fresh again.'

'C'mon. Kids are always fresh . . . '

'Joycie sneaked out a couple of hours ago and left Lucy at home by herself. So Lucy decided she was going to cut all the flowers off my geranium plants. She thought they smelled funny. Now that's fresh. That's more than fresh. She's growing up to be a hoodlum. It'll be smoking cigarettes and stealing cars next.'

'Lil, she's four, she can't drive. I don't think she's hoodlum material yet.'

'They start young, believe me. This neighbourhood is going down hill. It's not like this in the countryside.'

Dot laughed. 'Here we go again – peace and quiet with the cows. C'mon, Lil, I'm sure there's hoodlums out in the sticks too.'

'Not so many bad influences, and you know who I mean.'

'C'mon, Lil. He just sits in that room all day, painting stuff. How's that a bad influence?'

'The drinking. You keep forgetting about the drinking. You should see what he did to that nice roast of beef I had in the fridge.'

'What do you mean?' asked Dot.

'Chopped it all up. With a carving knife. And left the juice all over the floor. It wasn't a pretty sight.'

Dot shivered. 'Chopping stuff up with a knife? That *is* a little strange,' she said nervously.

'And he isn't exactly popular with the neighbours,' Lil continued. 'You know what he did a couple of days ago?'

'What?' Dot asked.

'You know the big red, white and blue "Victory" banner the Murphys put outside the front of their grocery shop last week when it was announced that the war was over?'

'Yeah,' Dot answered.

'Well, it seems old Pops took one look at the banner, went into the shop and started talking German to Tim and Ginny Murphy.'

'You're kidding,' Dot gasped. 'When they just found out for sure that young Davey was killed over there?'

'Yep,' Lil said grimly. 'He was drunk of course, but that didn't stop Ginny from calling me up in hysterics that evening, accusing us of keeping a Nazi under our roof.'

Dot looked sympathetic.

'It's been bad enough the last few years trying to explain to people why Max wasn't signing up like the rest of his friends. The Government may say that telecommunications is an essential industry during war time and that Max has been doing his bit for the war effort right here at home – but your neighbours don't always feel the same way.'

'Well, your good friends all understand,' Dot said, and patted Lil on the arm.

'And then we get landed with Max's crazy father who goes around speaking German when he wants to rile up the neighbours.'

'And then people go and throw rocks through our window,' Lucy piped up from the corner.

'You mind your own business and watch that wall,' Lil snapped.

Lil dropped her voice as Pops walked down the stairs. 'Well, there he goes,' said Lil. 'Out for more booze, I'll bet.'

Pops went out the front door and down the street.

'What can you do?' Lil continued. 'Drunk every day and the old goat is seventy-five. Jeez, you think he'd be dead by now.'

'People can surprise you,' Dot shrugged.

'Nothing surprises me,' said Lil. 'That old goat will live longer than me.'

Pops had an idea that the motorcycle was going to run the light. I've got the green, he thought stubbornly as he walked across the street. I've got the green, it's my right of way. He walked, resolutely, looking straight ahead.

Diamonds in the Window

Mr Barthelmus had a small but distinguished jewellery shop on the corner of Maple and Main, and Joycie used to swing past it every day after school so she could have a quick survey of the stuff in the window. Every Saturday morning, Joycie was down at Barthelmus Fine Jewellery Shoppe just before it opened, eyeing up the diamond rings in the window. Joycie allowed herself the pleasure of trying on a selection of rings each weekend, and spent a good hour savouring this pleasure before going on to weekend pursuits more typically followed by the average fifteen-year-old.

Joycie had her Saturday fitting expeditions down to a T. She knew exactly how long Mr Barthelmus would tolerate her window-shopping before he got a little touchy. She also knew exactly how to flatter him so she got the most out of her sixty minutes.

'Oh, look at that!' she would exclaim. 'Isn't that the most beautiful ring you have ever seen in your life!'

Joycie would point at a particular diamond as if it were the biggest, most delectable crème-chocolate ever and roll her eyes and lick her lips in anticipation. 'You have such good taste, Mr Barthelmus,' she would coo. 'Where do you find such beautiful rings?'

Mr Barthelmus was a real sucker for flattery and Joycie's act got him every time. Before he knew it, he was pulling out this tray and that tray and Joycie was holding up her left hand and admiring this ring and that ring in front of the special modelling mirror he kept on the counter.

'Really, Sidney,' Pat his wife would tut, whenever she popped in from their house which was connected to the shop. 'Really. Why on earth do you waste so much time on a fifteen-year-old kid? You know Lil doesn't want her in here mooning over the rings all the time. It's not healthy. She's only a kid. Don't encourage her.'

'C'mon, Pat,' Sidney would say, spreading his hands real wide and looking up towards the ceiling. 'C'mon! There's worse things a fifteen-year-old could be doing on a Saturday morning. What's the problem with her trying on a few rings? She might be a customer in a couple of years.'

Pat would just make this little snorting noise and walk through the back door into their house. 'That's a lot of selling for the sake of one ring,' she would mutter, and slam the door shut behind her.

At about 10 a.m. every Saturday, Joycie would reluctantly wedge the last ring back into its tray and say, 'Well, they're all very nice, Mr Barthelmus, but none seem quite right. I'll stop by next week. Maybe you'll have the one then. Thank-you!' Joycie would saunter out the door and Mr Barthelmus would tend to the less intrepid jewellery connoisseurs who arrived in the shop later.

Joycie had known exactly what she wanted from life at the age of four. She was an ambitious child and extremely competitive. Hopscotch was a prime example of this. Joycie was naturally good at games and ruthless to boot. Whichever square was her target, the stone would land dead-centre on the number. If another stone was on the square she needed,

Joycie would knock it off with one quick flick of her wrist. Joycie was a girl with a plan: she would hop, skip, and jump her way up in the world. If anyone got in her way, all the situation needed was a little wrist action.

Joycie's plan was a simple one – she would be married by the age of eighteen and married to the most eligible bachelor possible. Eligible meant wealthy, hard working, prestigious, and conventionally handsome. She'd had enough of blue-collar living – her husband's collar would be whiter than white. She would leave Philadelphia far behind and move into a wonderful house in the suburbs. Into a place that had everything. All the dreams that people ever looked for. And she would get them. She would get them *all*.

The Stitzengers supported Joycie's plans wholeheartedly. In fact, they started encouraging her and advising Joycie on the right sort of husband the day after she started walking.

'A pretty girl like you will have the boys lining up for you. You'll be a heartbreaker.'

'You won't have any trouble finding a good man, with looks like yours.'

'A rich husband, that's what you want.'

'You don't want to have to struggle through life like we did.'

'It always helps to plan ahead in life, young lady. Plan ahead and work for what you want. That's the key to success. That's the American way.'

'In America,' they would say. 'In America if you work hard, you can get what you want.'

Joycie did work hard. She started planning her wedding as soon as she could. It started with crayon drawings of her wedding dress – different variations for each season, just to be on the safe side. Soon she had the names for the kids (Veronica and Jeffrey) and the dog (Muffy) picked out.

As soon as she hit high school, Joycie started trying on rings.

'They say diamonds are a girl's best friend,' she would tell Susie, her best friend at that point. People judge you on the type of ring you wear – it has to be tasteful, not gaudy, but big enough to show that you're going places in life. I want a diamond I can rely on. I want a diamond I can trust.' Joycie would then give Susie this diamond-hard, significant look. Susie would always get this nervous feeling and wonder if Joycie had decided that Susie had done something truly horrible and that Susie's days as the best friend of Rushmore High's most popular freshman were well and truly numbered.

After all those years of preparation, Joycie suffered a sort of stage-fright the week before her senior prom. It was set for 10 June 1957 and was destined to be the second most important day of her life. Joycie thought of the senior prom as sort of a dress rehearsal for her wedding. Of course, Joycie was going with John Trumball, the best-looking football player at Rushmore High. But Joycie suddenly doubted whether the dress she had bought six months ago, after weeks of pleading with her mother, was the *right* dress. Sure, it looked nice, but nice wasn't quite enough. The way Joycie looked at it, her future depended on this prom. She dragged her mother to Monique's Dress Shop and showed her the big white dress in the window; the white dress with the satin bodice and the big frothy skirt buoyed up with layers of tulle and sprinkled with shiny silver spangles.

'Look, Mother,' she breathed. 'Isn't it beautiful? Monique says it's all the way from Paris. Isn't it perfect?'

'It looks like a wedding cake,' Lil said doubtfully.

'What's wrong with that?' Joycie asked. 'It's sort of symbolic, right?'

'I guess,' Lil answered.

'Well?' said Joycie.

'Well, what?'

'Well, can I have it?' Joycie said this quickly, almost under her breath.

'What?' Lil looked at her like she was crazy. 'What? What about that perfectly good, never-worn, "this-is-the-most-beautiful-dress-I-have-ever-seen-in-my-life" hanging in your closet?' Lil was almost shouting. Joycie burst into tears.

'Do you think we have money to burn, young lady?'

'It's only a hundred dollars,' Joycie sobbed.

The tears didn't help. Lil slapped Joycie and dragged her home, howling her eyes out.

Joycie did wear the white wedding-cake dress to the prom – or almost. Lil had copied down the design and sewn the whole thing from memory for less than half the price. Lucy, Joycie's younger sister, would have to wear the pale yellow gown after it had been packed away in mothballs for two years.

Joycie was putting a final spritz of hairspray on her hair when the doorbell rang. John was right on time. Joycie floated down the stairs, her white skirts billowing around her like sails on a ship. She went to the door, but Max got there first.

'What time will you be back?'

'About midnight, Daddy.'

'Is he a safe driver?' Lil asked, joining Joycie and Max near the door.

'Yes, Mother.' The doorbell chimed again and Joycie reached for the doorknob. Max blocked her way.

'Who is this boy?'

'John Trumboll. You've met him before, Daddy. He's

waiting outside – can we let him in?' She pulled at the door and Max pushed it shut again. The doorbell rang, a question.

'What are his plans for after high school?' Lil asked.

'He's going to be a lawyer. Mother, this isn't the time to talk about all this!'

'Don't be fresh with your mother, young lady. It's never a bad time to talk about prospects.'

'You don't want to make a mistake. You want a career man so you don't have to struggle for the rest of your life,' Lil advised.

'I worked hard to get where I am, young lady, and it wasn't easy.' Max thumped his chest for emphasis. 'Now we have a nice house in a nice neighbourhood. Think about it when you're young. We've given you all the things we never had.'

'And want to see you get on in life,' Lil added.

The doorbell went again, more persistently. Max pulled the door open and shouted to a bewildered young man, 'Hold your horses! I'm just having a word with my daughter!' and promptly shut the door again. Joycie groaned, caught in a verbal tennis match.

'It's important to settle down and get yourself a good husband,' Max pointed out.

'One that doesn't drink.'

'And doesn't smoke.'

'And none of this divorce business – you wouldn't know where's he's been,' Lil said, wagging her cigarette at Joycie.

Joycie nodded frantically and made another grab for the door. Max pushed it shut again. 'And make sure he works hard—'

'No, make sure he's rich so neither of you have to work hard,' Lil corrected.

'That's hard work,' Max said knowingly to Lil.

'That's right,' she answered.

The doorbell chimed once more, hesitantly. Max opened the door and yelled at Joycie's date. 'All right! Have some respect! What's your hurry, is there a fire or something?'

Joycie slipped under Max's arm and out the door. She was halfway down the walkway before she yelled goodbye.

Max and Lil had a feeling of *déjà vu*. They were standing by the front door thinking that it only seemed like months ago that Joycie was on her way to the prom. But it was two years later – 1959. And Joycie had just announced that she was about to get married. She faced them, her arm linked through Joe's.

'Aren't you going to congratulate us?' Joycie looked expectantly, back and forth.

'Congratulations,' Lil said.

'Many happy returns,' Max added.

'Come on, honey, our dinner reservation is for eight o'clock.' Joe extended his hand to Max and Lil and shook heartily. Joycie kissed them both goodbye. As the door closed, Lil and Max leaned back against it, tired.

'What do you think?'

'He's divorced, Lil.'

'Well, he's rich.'

'But he's divorced.'

'He doesn't smoke.'

'He drinks! Drinks like a drowning fish!' Max waved his arms.

'But he works hard. And he's nice to her.'

'Yeah, but—'

'No buts, Max. I make it three out of five and that's pretty good odds.'

'But not perfect.'

'Max, not even you are perfect.'

'Close enough though. Right?'

'You might just be right there, mister,' Lil said smiling.
'You might just be right.'

Neon, Pennsylvania

It's all a question of balance, of finding that place between standing and falling . . . like a marsh bird perched near the water's edge with one leg tucked up into its feathers. But suddenly, *unexpectedly*, the balance can slip sideways. Arms flail, legs wobble, and everything comes tumbling down, a death spiral towards chaos.

Tilda Hegarty was putting a jar of pickled cucumbers on the top shelf of the pantry. She'd done it a million times before, but for some reason her concentration wasn't there. Tilda was thinking of this and that, feeling all daydreamy in the dry August air, listening to the leaves rattling above the house, almost hearing the clouds move. She slid the stepladder towards the far wall of the pantry and started climbing up, holding the jar of pickled cucumbers in her hand.

Normally her balance was pretty good for a woman of seventy. She had climbed that stepladder in the pantry so many times, it was an old habit. But suddenly the ladder started wobbling and she teetered. She could feel the air move under her in directions she wasn't used to, but at the same time she went all sleepy and started thinking of the strangest things. She clutched the jar to her to stop it from breaking, forgetting to throw her arms in a direction calculated to slow down or stop her fall.

She could see the ceiling wheel up over her slowly, and caught her breath as she saw the lights of Philadelphia, then a vast stretch of cornfield sweep over the top of her. She watched, half frightened, half curious, as she saw Tinicum float above her, then around her – the Tinicum of almost fifty years ago, back in 1908 . . .

She could see Jack driving their old battered second-hand car up the dusty road that led to their house. And there she was sitting next to him on the front seat, bounced around by every bump in the road and trying to hold a ridiculous summer hat on her head. They had no money to go anywhere special, so their honeymoon was their first night in their new place. They got out of the car and stood looking at the ramshackle house and the old sign that hung creaking over the front porch. 'Elephant Inn', it read.

They stood laughing and making jokes about the sign until the McFarlands who ran the post office directly across the street came out to see what all the commotion was about. They all shook hands and Mr McFarland started telling Jack and Tilda his weather predictions for the month ahead. But his wife dragged him away before turning to Jack and Tilda and saying, 'Come and have some supper with us later tonight. I'm sure you've got plenty to do.'

'Sure do, ma'am,' Jack smiled. As soon as the McFarlands were out of sight he grabbed Tilda clean off her feet and carried her through the screen door into their new place. 'Welcome to Pachyderm Palace,' he said.

. . . For a split second she could see the side wall of the pantry tilt alarmingly near her head and jars of tomatoes hovering just in front of her eyes. Everything moved slowly, so very slowly. She stretched one hand towards the wall and thought, This is what it feels like to be flying . . .

Tilda could see another summer, maybe twelve years later, and there was Eloise just ten years old sitting on the porch swing, flicking through the magazines she had made Tilda order through the grocery shop. Magazines featuring beautiful models in expensive clothes, famous theatre actresses in New York City, and stories all about that fast-growing, glamorous place called Hollywood. 'Look,' Eloise would say, indicating tinted photographs of pastel buildings surrounded by palm trees, 'it's summer there all year round and everyone has lots of money. I'm going to live there some day.'

Tilda would laugh and say, 'Pretty pictures are one thing, but money doesn't grow on trees. Not even in California.' Eloise would just swing back and forth on that porch swing, ignoring everything Tilda said. She would watch the dusty road out front, seeing something there that she couldn't find in the big rows of corn that stretched like the Atlantic Ocean out towards the edge of the world.

. . . She could feel her fingertips touch the cool glass of the tomato jars, slip down past the labels marking the year they were put up. Her feet were lifting higher, floating slightly above her head and her skirt was billowing open, the way she imagined a parachute would . . .

Eloise hated Tinicum. When she turned fifteen she started dressing as much like the city women in her magazines as she could. She would make these outfits with fabrics bought on special order from the shop and would send away for hats and shoes and gloves from the Sears and

Roebuck catalogue. Eloise would work in the shop all day, serving the farmers who had driven for miles for their groceries or the truckdrivers who stopped in for a cold drink. Tilda would watch Eloise laugh as the truckdrivers told her stories about their travels across America. They would lean close to her, whispering those stories in Eloise's ear and she would smile and laugh, her pretty face shaded from the sun in a big hat copied from a magazine.

. . . As she floated down towards the floor, the sun slipped in from the tiny window in the left wall of the pantry, catching her just in the eyes. It was strange, dazzling, erasing all the jars, bottles and bags of things around her . . .

It wasn't long before Eloise started trying to find out more about all those stories the truckdrivers used to tell her. Tilda would wake up at night, hearing the click of the screen door, unnaturally loud in the quiet of Tinicum at midnight. She would look out the window and see two shadows moving fast down the road and catch the sound of laughter floating up towards the window. Eloise and some man running off towards Neon, a place about four miles down the road. Neon wasn't much of a place, more a collection of three neon signs spelling out 'GAS', 'ED'S' and 'NEON' on the edge of a dark stretch of cornfield lapping up against the dirt that was Tinicum Pike.

Rumour had it that Neon, Pennsylvania was the home town of the man that invented those lights that kept places like New York City up all night. Some people had big dreams for the place, but those visions seemed to just disappear into the surrounding cornfields. An anonymous entrepreneur with a hankering for getting out of Philadelphia and setting himself up as mayor of a spanking new town had given the place its name. He had started the rumour about the mysterious inventor. But some big plans never work out and the would-be mayor left the town to its own devices and went off to try his luck as a bootlegger.

Neon never was much of a place. Just a gas station and Ed's, a place that sold homemade beer during Prohibition. It started out as a barn where people sat at makeshift tables and anyone could bring out a guitar or fiddle to get people dancing. Eloise told Tilda all about it when she lay in bed one morning, her head (she said) just about splitting in two. 'It's wonderful,' she told her mother. 'Everyone knows me there and they all say I'm the most beautiful girl they've ever seen. It's like being famous.'

. . . The look of the world changes when you see it with your head so far below your feet. Her left arm touched the floor first, but her right hand kept hold of that jar of pickles, protecting the glass like a new born baby. She thought, This is what it's like to be dying. Everything goes so slowly . . .

Eloise disappeared one day, just after she turned seventeen. She left a note on the breakfast table apologizing for not having time to do her chores, but she had a ride to California and was going to go and try to get herself a screen test. Jack stood at the window, just staring down Tinicum Pike for a few minutes. 'I know that bastard's face,' he said quietly. 'If anything happens to our little girl, I'm going to make sure I find a way to kill him.'

They did their best not to worry and stuck all the postcards Eloise sent them on to the kitchen wall. 'California is beautiful,' she wrote on the back of a card with a lot of palm trees on it. 'I'll buy you a house out here when I'm famous.'

*　　*　　*

. . . Her back came to a rest on the floor while her legs balanced precariously against the drawers under the cupboard shelves before slipping sideways towards the rest of her. She felt nothing. She listened to the clouds moving and watched what seemed to be the leaves rattling, as the sun shimmered the dust that floated up over her . . .

The screen door squeaked open one evening, just about supper time. They could hear a car pulling away down Tinicum Pike. Eloise sat down carefully, balancing herself and cradling her belly in that odd way that pregnant women acquire.

They didn't ask any questions. They were just glad to have Eloise home alive and well. Jack and Tilda weren't really too sure that they wanted to know what had happened. 'Hollywood isn't an easy place,' Eloise would say. They would just shake their heads, pretending that they understood completely. That they understood exactly what Eloise had gone looking for and what had happened to her along the way.

Greta was born just at the end of a hot July in 1928. She was named after some movie star Jack and Tilda had never heard of. But Eloise was never quite the same after she came home. She seemed to give up all talk of Hollywood, but she still wore beautiful clothes, perfectly matched dresses and shoes. She would work all day in the shop, quiet and patient like she was waiting for something to happen.

The Depression hit America, but the Hegartys didn't do too bad compared to most people. Truckdrivers still came their way and Eloise would serve them beer in bottles. They would whisper stories in her ear and she would smile and listen, but never said much back to them. They would smile, wave and whistle at Eloise as they drove away down Tinicum Pike. Eloise would sit on the porch swing, looking after them, not saying anything, just watching the road.

It's funny how things turn out. Tilda remembered it all so well. Strange memories of hot, long days of summer, time wrapping everything up and every change causing a big commotion.

Greta left home at seventeen in a big truck with a boy called Hank Weatherby. Eloise faded away even more after that. Wrestling alone with your memories isn't an easy thing. 'Everything seems to disappear,' Eloise would say. 'It's like those stretches of water that appear in the road on a hot day. They shimmer before you like some kind of promise and then disappear like ghosts when you reach out to touch them.'

Elvis Was a Hero

He reached for the wrench, but it slid and skittered just out of reach across the garage floor. Rusty rolled on to his back, took a few breaths with his eyes closed, then emptied a can of Bud down his throat. Lucy placed another can on the floor, just touching his cheek, then picked up the wrench and balanced it on top of the empty beer can.

'Thanks, hon,' Rusty grinned.

'It's OK.' She lit a cigarette, took one long drag on it, then put it in Rusty's mouth. She was lighting another as she walked back inside.

Rusty smoked the cigarette, half-looking over Ted's bike, still half-smiling about Lucy. That woman had timing – you could hit a curve, unexpected like, maybe 90 miles an hour, and she wouldn't bat an eye. Just lean into it exactly right, balancing like a bird or something, part of the bike, like a figurehead on a ship.

Rusty stubbed out the cigarette on the concrete, then took a long swig of beer before turning back to the bike. Rusty was in his element; he understood every inch of a bike and could just about take one apart and put it back together with his eyes closed. But Rusty knew no one who thought he was too smart – no one ever had. That was part of the reason he had left school on his sixteenth birthday, lied about his age, and joined the Navy. Now they had ads on TV saying, 'Don't drop out – get a high school diploma ... *get a job.*' There was a kid, maybe sixteen, in the ad cleaning windows and pumping gas and looking enviously at all the sporty cars that pulled into the station. Rusty thought he understood what the ad was trying to say – only morons worked in gas stations and it didn't really count as work because you had to be smart to work. Rusty thought there was some kind of problem with the thinking behind this ad. If you were smart, maybe you'd be smart enough to know how not to work?

The summer of 1959 was just beginning when Rusty got out of the Navy. He started working in a gas station as a mechanic. He had done his share of pumping gas when he was still at school, but where words and numbers used to jumble up in his mind and set his head spinning, all the pieces of a car or motorcycle would slip right into place, just naturally. 'You've got it, kid,' they'd all say. 'You're a poet with a tool kit. A grease monkey of a poet.' He'd just grin and say, 'Thanks.' He didn't have much of a way with words, wasn't much good at telling jokes or small talk, but everyone seemed to like him. Rusty was an easy going guy.

The only thing Rusty used to worry about sometimes was Lucy. He just couldn't figure out what a woman like her saw in him. He wasn't real smart, not like her anyway, and wasn't the ambitious type. Lucy didn't seem to mind that, but her old man sure did. That's why they had eloped. Her old man was always all right with him at Sunday dinner and all. They would talk about cars and bikes, anything with an engine. Her father had been an electrician's apprentice at thirteen – he was a man who was good with his hands. But he wanted something better for his daughter, and Rusty wasn't that something. So they decided to elope. Lucy thought it all out.

'Just take that painter's ladder from the Mulligans' house and sneak it over to ours on Monday night. Monday's a good night 'cause Daddy is down the neighbourhood bar and Mother is playing cards with the girls. I'll be watching TV. All you have to do is put that ladder up to my window and climb up. It's a cinch.'

'But why the ladder? If everybody's out, why can't you just walk out the front door?' Rusty asked.

Lucy looked at him like he was crazy, then said, 'If we're gonna elope, we gotta do it right. You have to use a ladder. Don't you ever go to the movies? Don't you ever watch TV?'

Rusty shut up fast. He spent so much time working on bikes, he never really watched much TV. And he sure didn't get to the movies, unless Lucy dragged him there. He knew he didn't know much about stuff like that, so he kept quiet and hoped Lucy wouldn't ask too many questions.

Rusty and Lucy had met a year ago in June 1959 at Flannegan's Bar in Philadelphia. It was the night of the junior prom, but Lucy and her friend June had decided to skip the prom, sneak off to a bar and try out their fake ID. Rusty remembered seeing them come in the door – their prom dresses were so wide, they had to tilt them sideways to get inside. Rusty thought Lucy was the prettiest thing he had ever seen.

The bouncer started giving the girls trouble about their fake ID, but they kept insisting they were twenty-one and their names were Mary and Clare. Rusty decided to help them out. He stepped up and said. 'Hey, there you are! You're late, Mary. It's OK, fella, this is my girl Mary and her sister Clare.' The bouncer kind of smiled and waved them inside.

'Thanks a lot,' June said with a big smile.

'Yeah, thanks,' Lucy added after lighting a cigarette.

Rusty didn't know what to say next. 'Where'd you get the cards?' he asked.

'Oh, they're my sisters',' June answered.

'But we're almost twenty-one,' Lucy emphasized.

'Yeah,' June said a little too fast.

Rusty didn't bother bringing up the subject of the prom dresses. He also didn't mention that he wasn't quite legal himself – he and Walter were celebrating their last week in the Navy and used their uniforms to get in the bar. Rusty had learned early on that no one asked for ID when you turned up in a uniform. 'First class service for the Services', they would say and usher them in the door. So Rusty left things as they were and just introduced the girls to his friend Walter.

'Pleased to meet you,' said June. She sat down next to Walter right away.

'You want some beers?' Rusty asked.

'Sure.'

Rusty took his time at the bar and tried to think up some things to talk about besides motorcycles and cars.

But most of the talking was done by June that night. She and Walter really hit it off and Rusty felt a little awkward. He went into the Gents to give himself a pep talk and comb his hair. Rusty's hair was his one vanity: it was dark, almost black, and styled like Elvis's. He combed his hair and wondered what Elvis would do in this situation. Just be cool, he thought. Elvis would get the girl, but he would play it cool. Rusty went back to the table and found that the band had started up and it was pretty hard to have a conversation anyway.

'Do you want to dance?' Rusty asked Lucy.

'Sure,' she said.

The band, The Chevys, were pretty good and did all kinds of rock and roll numbers, but without any instruments. They were dressed in matching light blue suits, and the lead singer Pete would croon all the lyrics while the other members of the band would sing the baseline, special sound effects, and backing vocals. They had this dance routine going and their stuff was pretty easy to step out to. Rusty and Lucy moved well together and spent the rest of the evening on the floor, looking like extras out of a movie, Lucy in her big yellow prom dress and Rusty in his Navy uniform.

It was two in the morning when he drove Lucy home, her big yellow dress flying all over the place as she perched behind him on his motorbike. Rusty waited with the bike while Lucy went up to her door. He could just about hear her parents ask, 'How was the prom?' before the front door shut behind Lucy. Rusty felt happy; he thought he probably looked a little bit like Elvis, leaning on his motorbike, black greased-back hair glistening in the moonlight. Rusty tried to remember a love song to sing on his way home, but had to settle with humming along with his motorcycle.

Rusty and Lucy spent most weekends together while she finished her last year in high school and he started the job at the garage. He had to admit that the Navy had been pretty good to him. When he signed up at sixteen Rusty had this idea that he'd get a chance to work on some interesting equipment in the Navy, and he'd been right. He'd learned a lot during those four years in the Service, and on his first Monday as a civilian landed his job at the garage. Rusty had no real regrets about being a high-school dropout. Lucy wasn't all that interested in sticking out school either, but there was no way her parents were going to let her quit early.

'You can't get nowhere without a high-school education,' her father would say. 'There's more to this world than riding around on the back of a motorbike.'

Lucy would roll her eyes and blow a steady stream of smoke rings towards the dining-room lamp. Rusty always felt a little awkward when this topic came up during dinner-time conversation and kept quiet about his own lack of a diploma. That was why he didn't need much convincing when Lucy suggested that her family wouldn't take too kindly to them getting married and that they'd better elope.

'My father is a little funny,' she said, 'about the idea of me marrying a guy just like he was. I think it would be easier if we just eloped, then let him get adjusted to it all later.'

So, on July 2 1960, a Monday night at about 9 p.m., Rusty climbed over the fence and sneaked through the Mulligans' backyard and grabbed the ladder propped up against the house. He wasn't sure about the best way of carrying the thing by himself, but somehow managed to grab it in the middle and balance it over his head while walking through the Mulligans' backyard. When he reached the fence, he realized there were going to be some problems. After a little stumbling and quiet swearing, he managed to get the ladder over the fence and through the Fredericks' yard, over another fence and through the Bowens' place and finally through a hedge of forsythia bushes before he propped that ladder up against the Stitzengers' house. Rusty remembered the stories his mother used to tell him about Prince Charming and wondered where he had gone wrong. He knew with a bone-shivering certainty that Elvis would never be caught dead in a situation like this.

'Lucy!' he called as quietly as he could. 'Hey, Lucy!' A light flicked on in the Bowens' house and Rusty started getting even jumpier. 'Lucy, I'm here!'

Rusty felt relief when her window slid up and Lucy stuck her head out. 'Well, c'mon, climb up!'

'You really want me to carry you down?' Rusty asked her. Lucy sighed. 'I explained it all before, didn't I?'

Rusty looked worried and Lucy started to get even more impatient.

'OK, I'm coming up,' Rusty stammered as he started climbing. He was just about at the top when Lucy balanced herself on the edge of the window. Something went wrong and Rusty felt a swaying and a lurch deep in his stomach, then this feeling of flying, like being on a motorcycle, but backwards, and then the crash as they fell into the forsythia hedge. The Bowens' house lit up like a Christmas tree. Rusty lay there, watching the lights spin while half-listening to somebody explain, 'The cat was on the roof and we were trying to get her down . . . '

As soon as everything settled down Rusty and Lucy climbed on the bike, which he had parked halfway around the block, and headed out on the highway towards New Jersey. They found the 24-hour Justice of the Peace that one of the guys at the garage had told him about and got hitched. It took exactly seven minutes. The Reverend Roger Jackson lived right next door to the Honeymoon Motel which was run by his wife Ruby, who witnessed the ceremony, then set them up with a first-class honeymoon suite in the motel.

'Congratulations, kids,' she said, and put Lucy's little bouquet of flowers into a glass of water. 'Don't worry, we won't wake you for breakfast!' She laughed real loud, slapping her big thighs, then closed the door firmly behind her.

Rusty and Lucy looked around the place, inspecting empty drawers, testing the shower for hot water, even seeing if the toilet flushed. Rusty was impressed by the big poster of Elvis hung on the wall opposite the bed. The King seemed to be watching them and smiling this nice kind of smile. Elvis, Rusty thought to himself, would know what to do at a time like this. Elvis is a hero.

Rusty and Lucy poked around the room a little more, then they bounced up and down on the bed a few times. 'Seem OK to you?' Lucy asked.

'Yeah. What do you think?'

'Seems OK. Hey! What's this?' Lucy pointed to a box on the bed's headboard that had '25 cents' written on it.

'I don't know. You want to try it out?' Rusty pulled a quarter out of his pocket. He slipped a look sideways to Elvis, but Elvis was still smiling that funny little smile and Rusty just sat there, hesitating.

Lucy reached over, took the quarter, slipped it into the slot, then pushed the button. The bed started vibrating like crazy. 'Wow!' Lucy yelled. 'How about that!' She rolled on to her back. 'Hey, not bad. Sort of like a massage or something.'

Rusty lay down next to her. 'Yeah, it's kind of like a slow cruise on a bike – but lying on your back.'

Lucy started humming this crazy song that buzzed and gurgled with each vibration of the bed. After a while they had a duet going that lasted until their quarters ran out. At three in the morning they fell asleep, exhausted and still dressed in their wedding clothes, with Elvis watching over them like an archangel in Heaven, all dressed in white and gold, and smiling like he was happy.

White Dresses

The house was quiet except for the wobbling buzz of a bluebottle throwing itself against the window glass. Emma readjusted the flowers which were beginning to wilt in the summer heat, then looked at the clock on the mantelpiece. Half past one: the service was due to begin at three. She wondered if Fred would be there, or if he'd be off drinking as usual with the disreputable characters that spent their time down around Cross Street.

Emma pulled back the curtains and looked at the sunlight glinting on the roofs and hitting all the glass in that peculiar way that dazzled the eyes. She could hear children playing somewhere down the road and a street car clanging in the distance. It was hard to believe that such a beautiful August could be so full of death. Doors had quarantine marks chalked on them, and the doctor scuttled endlessly around the neighbourhood looking worried and clutching his black bag like a crucifix. During the summer of 1922 diphtheria was an invisible poison that seeped through the air and slipped into the water.

Emma looked at Catherine, white dress lying as still and heavy as the lace curtains on the window. Emma smoothed an invisible wrinkle on the pure white. She had taken it out of tissue paper the other day and with a small twinge of sorrow, left it with the undertaker. Catherine lay there now, a fragile doll, too serious and silent in Emma's lacy wedding dress.

Seventeen years previously Emma's sister Mary had made her the dress. She remembered walking carefully in her white shoes, wobbling slightly on the heels and trying not to trip over the fluttering satin. She had felt like a tiny sailboat, skimming across the Delaware Bay, moving relentlessly towards the ocean which would take her in its big hands and crush her into tiny fingerings of driftwood.

Her father's lips were pressed together and unsmiling under his large walrus moustache. Her mother cried, but she cried at all weddings and Emma didn't read much more into it than that. Emma could still remember the feel of the ring slipping slowly, reluctantly down her finger, and the coolness of Fred's kiss surrounded by a cloud of rum. During the reception, when her brother Andy's band struck up the first dance for the couple to lead the way with, Fred's calloused fingers pressed hard into her waist and crushed her fingers until she was gritting her teeth with pain. But she led them through a reasonable waltz, smooth enough so that no one could accuse Frederick of being drunk.

Her parents bought them a small row house in Philadelphia as a wedding present and her father said, 'That's all you should be wanting from us. There's no need for you to come knocking at our door again.' Her parents did not approve of Fred's German origins, his life on the sea, his tattoos, his drinking, or his lack of religion. Fred had agreed to be married in a Catholic church, but that wasn't enough to raise his standing with her family. Mary reminded Emma that she should be grateful that her father had consented to give Emma a wedding, considering all the 'circumstances'. Mary was the only one who knew that Emma was pregnant, although Emma was fairly sure that her mother suspected. Mary did stand by her, even though her opinion of Fred was little higher than the rest of the family's.

Emma had met Fred at McNamara's Bar during the wedding party in honour of Bill McNamara and her friend Theresa. Emma's brother Andy knew Bill from school and his band was hired to play at the party. The McNamara wedding was a big event. Emma recognized a lot of people from school and church, and Bill had also invited all the bar regulars to join the celebrations. When Emma first noticed Fred, she had the feeling he had been watching her for quite a while. Emma's gaze was held by Fred's dark brown eyes which refused to let go. She looked at his blonde hair, the hard lines that formed his shape. His skin was tanned and had been etched by a salt-edged wind. She had never seen anyone like him before. Fred asked Emma to dance straight away. She paused before she stepped into his arms and captured the moment in her mind for ever. Fred pulled her backwards and forwards across the dancefloor – tide in, tide out. The sea-moon above them howled a drunken melody, a splashing song tangential to the clean smooth lines of reason.

Soon Fred began to court Emma and Mary usually went out with them as a chaperon. One sunny July afternoon, Mary sneaked away to see her own boyfriend and Fred borrowed a car and drove Emma out to the countryside for a picnic. Emma was certain that Fred would have asked her to marry him anyway, but realized that her tearful confession of pregnancy two months after the picnic hurried things along a bit.

At the beginning of their marriage Emma felt like she was navigating a dream. She spent most days fitting in pieces of furniture, polishing wood with wax, washing glass with vinegar until it sparkled. Soon she could feel the baby move inside her and spent more time sitting on the sofa reading a book, or she would go around to Mary's for some company. Fred was off on the ships for weeks at a time and was away for most of her pregnancy. She hadn't anticipated the loneliness that she felt. She would whisper quietly to the baby, telling it stories, counting the days until her birthing time, anxious for some company in their house that sang with emptiness.

Emma daydreamed through the sunlight and started having nightmares that set her tossing and turning in the darkness. In bad weather she had especially vivid nightmares where the sea would rear up into tremendous waves and crash down, swallowing a ship whose figurehead would scream from the water like a drowning harpy. She would wake up, covered in a thin dew of sweat, and would sit huddled on the sofa until morning, watching the light change and thinking she would die if Fred never came back. Emma wanted to explain this to Fred, to press her thoughts on to paper. Their whispers rattled in the night, but the words were lost, could not be excavated from her throat. She had nothing now but the small world within their house.

When Fred was away during that first year, he would send her letters full of drawings and little songs he made up whenever he stopped in a town for a while. Emma would poke her head into the post office every day and Mr Kelly would either raise his hands in resignation or sometimes wink, then wave her envelope like a prize. She would hurry home, rip open the letter and sit reading it over and over.

Catherine was born on 10 March 1905, exactly seven months after she and Frederick had been married. There was some talk, but it didn't seem impossible that Catherine had been born two months early. Her parents softened when they finally saw Catherine and let Emma come back to the house when Fred was away.

It was during their fourth year of marriage that things began to fall apart. Fred's temper seemed to sharpen and he would storm out of the house and go down to the bars around Cross Street at the smallest provocation. Fred wasn't home any more than before and they still couldn't find much to talk about when he was. Fred said it was hard to make a sailor settle down in a house. He also found it hard to cope with three children and a fourth on the way. Fred started to bring home bottles of rum and would sit listening to the radio, painting intricate designs on boxes for tobacco or snuff or a deck of cards. His friends would buy the boxes for some small change which kept his drinks tab paid.

Fred said he drank to keep the sea at bay. Long afternoons with the crawl of salt on the skin and sunlight prickling his clothes like a live thing left him feeling uneasy. In some ways he loved the freedom of working on the ships and he tried to kill that root of loneliness he had felt since he was a boy. Emma had seemed an answer, a wish, but something impossible to understand, and he began to hate her for it. He drew pictures of mermaids and sirens, and strange women from countries that never existed. He slept with women without names or places and sat in bars all night drawing pictures of fellow drinkers and playing cards. He seemed to have a charm with the deck and his winnings kept the children in clothes and the household running.

But Fred was a loner no one felt completely at ease with. He said strangers sniffed around him like suspicious dogs and snapped at his heels, which caused him to throw his fists at their throats. The more he drank, the more he took to brawling, but he never lost himself enough to get rolled and have his money taken off him. Fred stayed away longer as Emma had more children: Catherine, Betty, Alicia, Max,

Thea, Jimmy, Joe, Maureen, Tim, Peggy, and another on the way. He had no interest in children. They reminded him of growing up in a small town, being stuck in a small place, being a person without freedom. He felt like a figurehead on a ship who knows she's headed straight for the rocks. But he kept straight on course, disregarding all bad omens, almost willing the anger of the sea to crush everything he couldn't explain within him and leave him floating somewhere in the undertow.

Emma stood staring at Catherine's face and could see much of Fred in her features. Emma had tried to understand Fred, but never got very far except for realizing that she couldn't be more different than Fred. She loved children and, like some of the other women in her family, had an uncanny knack for pregnancy. Eleven children in seventeen years seemed to age Emma in a peculiar way. She remained slight and her face showed few lines at forty, but her movements were slow and her mind seemed somewhat adrift. She knew this would be her last pregnancy and wondered if death in the house would leave a mark on the baby.

On those rare occasions when Fred kissed her she could remember that summer day lying in the wildflowers. She could almost smell the cut grass from the nearby farm and feel the movement of the living things on the hillside under her back. In that suffocation of roses, she remembered being surprised at the contrast between the softness of the skin beneath Fred's shirt and his calloused hands and feet. There was nothing to think about, no questions to ask. Everything was right and she would hold a breathing picture of the time and place in her mind for ever. Fragile and perfect, she sheltered it under a globe of glass and refused ever to let it break.

Emma moved towards the mantelpiece and looked in the

mirror hanging above it. She examined the mark, shaped like a mauve butterfly, on her right cheekbone. She had asked Fred for some extra money to buy flowers, and his hand flew, then crashed against her face. She had reeled against the wall, instinctively shielding her belly with her hands, but he had gone, the door slamming behind him. She had chipped some ice from the block and pressed it against the swelling.

Emma turned back to the mirror and could see, as if in slow motion, his hand as she had seen it come towards her again and again. Sometimes swirling through the dust that floated in front of the window; or refracted in the rectangle of mirror; or a dark shape skimming towards her from the periphery of her sight. It was never quite real, just fragmented – in black and white. Her face collapsing like a broken flower.

She never spoke about the thin bruisings that sometimes tattooed her skin. Not even when Mary or the children asked her directly. Once Max, their eldest son, came into the living room when she was crying. 'Did Pops do something to you?' he asked. Emma made up a little story, slipping around the subject like a sailboat on the smoothest of waters. It was only on rare days such as today that the quietness trickling through an empty house caused her to dwell on remembrances. And to wonder what had gone wrong.

The Caress

Eloise picked up her bag of groceries and jumped on the bus. It had been a warm day with a faint breeze that just rustled the palm fronds. She took a seat in the middle of the bus and arranged her purse and groceries around her.

She couldn't believe it. This was Hollywood. It looked exactly like the pictures in the magazines. Eloise lived in a room that she rented on the outskirts of town. It was a little seedy, but she made a point of going shopping in the nice parts of town – just in case some movie producer took a notion to discover her.

She watched the lights flick past the window and tried to imagine what her life would be like as a movie star. The people she saw were dressed like they knew what it was like to be famous. They strolled and laughed and had a good time.

The sky had just moved from deep blue to black and although it was mid-September, the weather was still quite warm.

Back home you would be able to taste a frost in the air. She tossed her hair away from the back of her neck. I like this, she thought. This is really the place to live.

Eloise mulled over the film she had just watched. There

didn't seem to be that much to it. Just learn your lines and make sure that you keep your best side to the camera. She could do that. Eloise was just dying to do a screen test. Any day now her life was going to change for ever.

The air was heavy – it prickled around Eloise's neck. She pushed her hair away from her skin and let the air circulate. She felt a slight tug on her hair and leaned forward to extricate it from the fingers of the passenger behind.

They were entering the dingier side of Hollywood. This part of the journey always made Eloise nervous. There weren't many street lights here. Sounds echoed in the empty streets and crept up through the darkness.

The person behind her accidentally tugged on her hair again. As Eloise leaned forward, the hand followed. She could feel someone stroking her hair – very gently, almost indiscernibly. For a moment she wondered if it was some-one she knew behind her, but then she remembered that she didn't know anyone in Hollywood. The person behind her started to twist their fingers in her hair. Eloise turned around abruptly and said, 'Stop playing with my hair.'

He was in his early twenties. He smiled and looked at her with eyes held wide open.

Eloise turned back to watching the window. She could feel him stroking her hair again. She didn't know what to do. Her stop was soon. She tried to ignore the touch until she overhead someone say, 'I've never seen a fondler on a bus before.'

'Move seats!' someone said loudly.

Eloise felt a hand slide down her arm. She shifted her purse closer to her lap. Fingers entangled themselves further into her hair.

'Move seats, lady!' she heard someone call out.

Eloise was confused. She turned around. 'Stop it,' she said.

The man just smiled and leaned towards her. His eyes were pale blue and his hair thin and fair. His hands gripped the back of her seat.

'Why don't you change your seat?' a man sitting towards the back questioned.

Everyone on the bus was looking at her, but most flicked their eyes away when she looked at them. Eloise felt dirty. She felt as if she had done something wrong. She pushed herself out of her seat suddenly and grabbed her groceries. She made her way towards the door. She prayed that he wouldn't follow her. It was a five-minute walk down a quiet, dark street from the bus stop to her tiny room. As soon as they stopped, she jumped off and hurried away. She looked over her shoulder – no one had followed.

Eloise walked down the street quickly, her breath coming in short, sharp bursts. She could still see his face, smiling slightly, eyes opened too wide, pale blue and unconnected. Eloise concentrated on breathing slowly and deeply so that the movement of air did not echo so loudly in the night. She pulled her keys out of her purse as she walked, and felt her muscles unclench with relief as she clicked up the steps to the little house where she rented a room. She moved her key towards the lock.

When he stepped out of the shadows he took her by surprise. 'You have a nice little room,' he said. 'I've always enjoyed watching you in your home.' With a movement she hardly saw he propelled her hand away from the lock. Her spine slammed against the house, each vertebra seeming to make a separate impact, each sliding across the rough wood. He pushed his face close to hers and reached up to touch her hair. As he twisted his fingers through it, her head was yanked back against the wall. She saw nothing but his pale blue eyes as he tore open the fabric of her dress. She felt nothing but the rough wood of the house and his fingers squeezing quiet the bubbles of a scream within her throat. She heard nothing but his voice close to her ear, describing in perfect detail each violent caress.

Caught Between Dreaming
and Morning . . .

Lucy keeps having the same dream. She doesn't remember when it started. It seems as if it has been with her forever. A warning, a memory, an entanglement of then and now.

Her heart is pounding and her body is covered with a thin residue of sweat.

She turns her head slightly and can see it.

The sunlight just catches the edge of it. First silver, a tailfin, then hardgloss cherry red. Its reflection flicks in and out of the wing mirror like a fish leaping tenaciously upstream.

Lucy looks left again – nothing, then up into the rear view mirror. There – the skittering of red weaving in and out of traffic. Furtive but fast, the red convertible is gaining on her every minute. She pushes the accelerator impatiently and the Mustang growls, chokes on a gear, then slips up to 80 m.p.h. as she swerves left to pass.

The car refuses to let her cut back in lane. It zigzags in front of her. Her eyes search the mirror and she sees a red fender nosing forward. Lucy skids, gravel flies, tiny hailstones clatter on the windshield. One stone ricochets hard and fast into the wing mirror.

She watches as the image splits and showers like atoms, multiplying: a hundred red convertibles screaming their dangerous reflection all around her.

II

Disturbia

＊＊＊＊＊＊＊＊＊＊＊＊＊＊＊＊＊＊＊＊＊＊＊＊＊＊＊＊＊＊＊＊

You will have a greater chance to be yourself than any people in the history of civilization.
— *House Beautiful*, 1953

We are moving ahead, but we are not moving ahead rapidly enough.
— John F. Kennedy, 1960 Presidential campaign

With ordinary automatics, you have to flip levers, twist dials, practically be a mechanic. With a Necchi, you just push a button . . .
— 1957 sewing machine advertisement

Isn't it better to talk about the relative merits of washing machines than the relative strength of rockets?
— Vice President Richard M. Nixon, the 'kitchen debate' in Moscow, 1959

Never before so much for so few.
— *Life* magazine, 1954

＊＊＊＊＊＊＊＊＊＊＊＊＊＊＊＊＊＊＊＊＊＊＊＊＊＊＊＊＊＊＊＊

The Odds Are Against It

Another place for sale. The sign looked pretty good. George Gardner had decided to put it about three yards behind the mailbox and about a yard to the left. That way it just nudged the right-hand edge of the picture window and didn't obscure any of the house's nicer features. And you could read it just fine from the road if you happened to drive past.

Lots of people were moving away from the neighbour-hood just then. George wasn't complaining – it was good business for him. He was just surprised, really. Tinicum was a pretty nice neighbourhood – quarter-acre lots, two-car garages, and a quiet block where kids could ride their bicycles without being run over. But the young couples that lived there would be offered a better job somewhere else, in some other State. And they would have to move. You have to think about your family.

George and his wife Brenda had lived in Tinicum for ten years. Their house was one of the first built and it over-looked the old farm house that had been there since 1785. Almost a monument, that house. George and Brenda watched all the houses spring up around them. Lots of families moved in. George helped most of them move in, being the real-estate agent and all.

Tinicum was a family neighbourhood. Three- or four-bedroom houses, mostly. When George showed a couple a house he always said, 'If you're planning a family, go for at least three bedrooms. Chances are you'll have two kids – maybe not at the same time, but maybe only a year or two apart. And you just can't know whether it will be two boys, two girls, or a boy and a girl. You can't predict for sure. And if it's a boy and a girl, you really should have three bedrooms. You'll want to decorate them different. Be prepared, go for three bedrooms. Kids are unpredictable.'

Sometimes they were worried about money, those young couples. They shuffled their feet a little and mumbled, 'Well, Mr Gardner, we just don't know. We don't know whether we can afford three bedrooms. Maybe we should look at two.' But George always said straight away, 'Listen, this is nineteen sixty-four. You have it good. They call this the space age in all the magazines. We have enough money to send people out in space. And everything's electric – dishwashers, washing machines, can openers, carving knives, toothbrushes. In nineteen sixty-four everything's efficient. And you can buy it, stores will give you credit. When I was young, it was different.'

George and Brenda couldn't afford three bedrooms when they were married in 1938. They couldn't afford a house. They had lived with Brenda's parents, before moving into a little apartment in Philadelphia. And they couldn't afford children. George had a lot of bad luck. Everyone he worked for kept going out of business. So George and Brenda waited on having kids. In 1954 George became a real-estate agent. The company gave him a special deal on a house. Four bedrooms. Brenda was over the moon.

'Let's have some kids,' she said. George thought it was

a good idea too. They started decorating the two smallest rooms.

The doctor wasn't too happy when Brenda finally became pregnant. 'You're forty-two years old, Brenda, and you need to lose some weight. I want to keep an eye on you. Forty-two is not the best age for having a baby. I want to see you regularly.'

The Gardners painted one room pink and one blue. Blue won the bet. Brenda was over the moon. She wanted to call the baby George – George Junior. Brenda didn't listen much when the doctor tried to explain that Georgie would need special care. 'Of course,' she snapped, a little annoyed. 'Of course he will.'

They got along all right. Georgie seemed to cry more than other kids. He had a temper on him. But Brenda didn't care one bit. A year later they had Martha. Lucky they had painted the other room pink.

The doctor had explained again that it was risky for George and Brenda to have another kid. Brenda merely said, 'We don't regret for one minute having Georgie. Besides, what are the chances of it happening again?'

'Pretty good,' the doctor had answered.

Martha was different. She was a little slow, but didn't have a temper on her. She was a real sweet baby. Never cried. Never threw things. Real sweet.

Nothing was too bad until Georgie went to school. He went to the same school as the other kids in the neighbour-hood, but attended a special class for the 'special kids'. Georgie used to lose that temper of his in school. Used to hit the other kids. He didn't really like the teacher much either. It was kind of hard when he started school.

But Martha was a real sweet kid. Would do anything you asked. Real quiet, real sweet. Still, none of the other kids in the neighbourhood would play with her. She'd come home crying some days. 'No one likes me,' she would say, and press her fists into her eyes to try to stop the tears from leaking out. Brenda would find the Crayolas and scribble all the colours in the box with her. For hours.

It was hard when Martha went to school too. Brenda started getting lonely. She would cry when Georgie and Martha had no one to play with. The kids started calling Georgie 'Teabag' at school. They said the brown marks on his skin looked like tea stains. Georgie used to cry, then scream and hit. He couldn't talk very well, but he could hit. He was big for his age.

It was hard on Georgie and Martha, not having any real friends. George understood that it was hard. You live in a neighbourhood for ten years, but you don't really have any friends. No one invites you round for lunch. No one says, 'Come to our barbecue this weekend.' No one asks you to play golf. You live in the same place for ten years, and it's like living nowhere in particular.

When Georgie and Martha were six and five years old, Brenda started talking about how much she loved kids again. 'Let's try one more time,' she pleaded. 'Let's try again. It's probably our last chance to have another baby. The odds are against it happening again.'

'Brenda,' George tried to explain. 'I don't think it works like that. It's not like gambling or chance or getting the same number on the wheel of fortune three times running. There are other factors. I think when you're older like us, your whole body gets a little tired. Worn out from too much work. Then it happens with the children. They end up a little slow, like us.'

Brenda didn't believe it would happen three times out of three. Brenda was an optimist.

* * *

George and Brenda moved into separate bedrooms when Cindy was born. It's not that I don't love Brenda, George reasoned with himself. I do. It's just that she's a real fighter and won't give up.

I do love Brenda, George thought every time he closed his bedroom door at night. It's just that Brenda doesn't know when to quit. Even when the odds are against her.

Baptism

Her stomach had flipped over and her head seemed to be spinning counterclockwise to the highway whirling around her. They leaned into the curve on the turnpike and the ground sprang up near her face in sudden sharp focus. Lucy's stomach flipped over again as she gripped Rusty's jacket tighter. This is it, she thought. This is death flying straight at me. This is the best thing I have ever done.

The road straightened out and they moved into formation almost by instinct, but mostly by hierarchy. JJ and Tina were first, followed by PegLeg and Jed doing crazy tricks. Rusty and Lucy rode in the middle, backed up by his better buddies Scooter and Pete. This was the first time that the Warlocks had asked both Rusty and Lucy to ride with them.

Rusty had done a particularly spectacular tattoo on JJ, and JJ was feeling magnanimous. 'You want to hit the beach with us?' he asked Rusty, casual-like. 'We're riding out of Philly about eight in the morning on Saturday and hanging out for a couple of days. Rile up the locals and all that shit.' JJ scratched his beard for a while and then said, kind of like it was an afterthought, 'You can bring Lucy.'

'Sure,' said Rusty. 'I'll see if she wants to come.'

Lucy wasn't sure about the idea. The guys were always polite when they turned up, but Lucy just couldn't get the headlines from the local paper out of her head. 'Devils in Disguise!' 'Madmen on Wheels!' 'Lock Up Your Daughters – The Barbarians are Coming!' People got nervous every time the Warlocks came to town.

Rusty had known Scooter in the Navy and they kept in touch when Rusty was working at the garage. Once a week or so, he and Scooter would hit a couple of bars and talk about motorcycles. Scooter had been crazy about them since he was a kid and his older brother had given him a few rides. 'Want a ride on the old scooter?' he used to ask him. After a while he just started saying, 'C'mon, Scooter boy, let's adios!'

Scooter spent most of his time on, around, or under motorcycles until he joined the Navy. He and Rusty became good buddies because Rusty understood Scooter's need to talk about the look of the road ahead, the floating and the dipping, the engine's sound, and the wind that just keeps going.

When Rusty and Lucy got married and moved into their place out in Tinicum, Scooter used to drop by every once in a while. Then he started to bring a couple of friends whose bikes needed fixing and began trying to convince Rusty that he should give up his job at the garage and just concentrate on motorcycles.

One day he brought along Pete, who had more tattoos swirling up his arms than anyone Lucy had ever seen. Rusty was really impressed and mentioned that he had learned to do tattoos when he was in the Navy. Somehow by the end of the conversation Pete was offering to swap Rusty an inking set for a complete overhaul on his bike. Rusty agreed and was soon inking fancy designs on the guys. 'You're a natural, Rusty,' they'd say. 'When it comes to tattoos and motorcycles, you're the best around.'

But when the guys from the Warlocks started rolling up to Rusty's garage pretty regularly, the neighbours started to gossip. The women would hide behind half-drawn curtains, peeping out every time they heard any kind of engine roar. They were jumpy with nervous excitement, almost anticipation, while complaining to each other about those wild men in leather with long hair, tattoos and all those muscles.

June finally brought the subject up during one of her coffee breaks with Lucy. 'People are gossiping about you and Rusty,' she said. 'All those motorcycles roaring in and out – people are saying you might be hippies or Communists or criminals, or something. They're talking about you more than Gloria Jameson right now.'

'Who do you mean by *they*?' Lucy asked.

'Well, everybody really. You know I went to that Avon beauty demonstration, and that's all anyone talked about. All those wild men growling up to your house and shaking up the neighbourhood. They watch everything from the window.'

'So we're not allowed to choose our friends?' Lucy asked.

'Oh, c'mon, Lucy. I'm only saying all this for your sake. It's no good if the neighbours won't speak to you.'

'OK,' said Lucy. 'Thanks. Thanks for telling me.'

Lucy brought up the subject while she and Rusty were having a couple of beers and watching TV. 'June says the neighbours are talking about us.'

'Why?' Rusty asked amiably.

'Because of all the guys from the Warlocks riding in and out. It makes them nervous.'

'Nervous?' Rusty repeated.

'Yeah – all the crazy helmets and beards and noise. I guess they think of them like Vikings or something. You know; rape, pillage and plunder.'

Rusty took another sip of his beer with a look of surprise stamped on his face. 'But the guys aren't dangerous or anything. They might be a little different than Walter or Bob or Jack. But they never start trouble – except maybe for PegLeg. Or JJ if you argue with him. Or maybe a fight or two in a bar . . .' Rusty paused, mulling it over, then looked at Lucy. 'I see what you mean. What if they just drop in one at a time, or quietly after dark?'

'Yeah, that's a good idea,' said Lucy. 'It's just that I don't want the other kids to start picking on Katie and Franky like they do with the Gardner kids. You know how kids act when other kids are different.'

'Yeah,' said Rusty. 'Pretty much like adults do when other people are different.'

Rusty had a word with the guys, who just laughed about the whole thing and agreed to calm down a little. Every once in a while PegLeg would lapse and roar around the neighbourhood doing wheelies and blowing kisses to the women watching from the windows. But he never got much more carried away than that.

On the road was another story though. The Warlocks would ride in formation and really take over. On a hot summer's day, as many as fifty bikes would be roaring out from Philadelphia, through the suburbs and down towards the Jersey shore.

They would play games with the motorists, pulling up close to the driver's window and smiling in, particularly if it was a good-looking woman. Sometimes a couple of bikes would surround a car and control the speed it could move at. But usually the Warlocks would just stream down the highway and cars would slip into the slow lane, jittery with the roar of so many engines.

When Lucy agreed to ride along with Rusty and the Warlocks for the first time, she felt a little strange. On the one hand it was like grabbing some forbidden freedom she had been looking for, and on the other hand she kept hoping that none of the neighbours would notice them going out to join the gang as they swept past Tinicum towards the shore.

But suddenly there they were, moving down the turnpike, faster than she had ever gone before. She could feel her blood doing strange things and her head felt light with the air whooshing under her scarf and around her face. The feel and smell of Rusty's jacket mixed with the growl of the engine, and she hoped her body would react to everything right and stay on the back of the bike.

They reached the shore after two hours of riding and a couple of short stops. It was only 10 a.m. and the sun was just starting to heat up the air and sand. Lucy took off her jacket and shoes and walked into the sea.

The cold pull of the undertow stirred sand around her ankles and disturbed her balance. She watched the water moving with its sense of urgency and felt the salt biting into the blister on the back of her heel. The ocean hurled itself towards her, time after time, then tugged persistently in retreat.

She finally fell towards the water with the tiredness and allowed the waves to baptize her with their roaring.

This is Where We Are Now

Bob Jameson was a jealous man. He knew it and didn't like the way his gut was so often tied up in a tangled mess. But he just couldn't hold back that great saltwash of feeling that left him with a need for something he didn't have. A need that tore his stomach into slivers.

Bob sneaked a look at Gordy Fisher who was jumping around with a paper plate attached to each ear. It's all one big holiday to him, Bob thought irritably as he poked the steaming hamburger unnecessarily for the fourth time. He doesn't know the meaning of hard work. There was a time when Bob had been sure Gordy was having an affair with his wife Gloria. The thought of Gloria with another man drove Bob wild, but he couldn't talk to her about it. Gordy used to hang around the Satellite Lounge and Bob heard rumours that Gordy and Gloria were seen there together. Bob watched Gordy and Gloria carefully whenever they talked to each other, but he couldn't detect any spark between them. Not like with Gordy and Amelia. But Bob still couldn't keep those knots out of his stomach.

'Hey, Bob!' Gordy shouted. 'Need a hand with those burgers?'

'I think I can manage a couple of burgers by myself, Gordy.'

'OK,' Gordy shrugged, and flapped his paper ears like the dwarf in Disney's *Snow White*. 'I'll just have another beer. Do you want a beer, Bob?'

'No,' Bob answered, stabbing a hamburger so hard he broke it in half.

Gordy shrugged again, then chased six-year-old Caroline Thompson around the swing set, trumpeting like an elephant and flapping his paper ears.

'Get her! Get her!' Tommy and Charlotte Jameson shouted. Gordy trumpeted again as Caroline squealed.

June laughed, then turned to Amelia Parkins and said, 'Gordy's so good with kids – he's a natural.'

'He sure is,' Amelia replied with a big smile.

'He'd make a great father,' June continued.

'I think so too,' Amelia said.

Gordy was now flapping the two paper plates near his mouth. 'Quack, quack!' he snapped and flapped at Katie and Franky. The kids were all in hysterics, rolling around on the lawn.

Jack Beaumont strolled over to the barbecue and handed Bob a beer. 'What's the matter with that guy?' Bob asked, pointing the long barbecue fork at Gordy.

'What do you mean?' Jack asked, before tipping some beer into his mouth.

'I don't know,' Bob grumbled. 'Just look at him. Can't keep away from the women.'

Gordy was standing in front of June Thompson, Gloria and Amelia. They were laughing as he punctuated some story with big gestures. Gordy didn't live in the neighbourhood. He was one of Walter Thompson's buddies from the golf club. He lived closer to Philadelphia in an apartment building that didn't allow children.

'They said it was a building for young professionals. I didn't realize that was another way of saying "No kids". Since when are the two mutually exclusive? I know lots of young professionals with kids.'

'But they probably live in a house, not an apartment, Gordy,' June retorted. 'I think you're living in one of those swinging singles' places.'

'Well, it's the quietest place for swingers in town, then,' he replied.

'Gordy, can I get you a hamburger?' Amelia asked.

'I'd love one if they're ready,' Gordy answered. Gordy seemed to change into another person when he talked to Amelia. His face lost its sharp edge, his eyes went all soft and his hands got nervous.

Amelia pushed herself out of the chair and moved towards the grill like a proud sailboat, her large bosom ploughing through the air like a ship's bow. Her dress billowed around her big haunches and sturdy legs, testing the direction of the breeze.

Bob put two hamburgers on the rolls Amelia had arranged on the paper plate. Beads of perspiration dotted her forehead and trickled along the creases of her thick, soft neck. Bob watched Amelia walk languidly back to Gordy. She handed him the hamburgers, then patted her wilting hairdo.

'Can you believe that?' Bob said to Jack. 'She's waiting on that jerk hand and foot.'

'I think we have a budding romance there,' Jack chuckled. 'They make a pretty nice couple.'

'*Couple?* What do you mean?' Bob looked at Jack furiously.

'Couple – you know, like one plus one.' Jack crossed his fingers to illustrate his point.

'Jesus, Jack. What about Phil?'

'C'mon Bob. Phil has been missing in action for almost three years now.'

'Missing is not the same as dead.'

'Missing in Vietnam probably is.'

Bob was about to contradict Jack, but thought better of it. They would just get into the same old argument and Bob would have to back down because Jack would point out that he had been to Vietnam, but Bob hadn't. Granted, Jack had gone as a West Point officer and had spent most of his time pushing paper in Saigon, but he had *been* there. He had a better, truer picture of what the war was really like.

Jack had the look on his face that usually accompanied his argument that began with: 'Three years missing in action means dead – or a prisoner of war. Would you want your wife to wait for ever, never knowing if you were going to come back?'

Bob was sinking into a worse mood. He ignored Jack's unspoken question and watched Gordy and Amelia while thinking about Phil.

Phil had been one of Bob's best buddies at college, where they both studied chemical engineering. Bob and Gloria were childhood sweethearts and were married as soon as Bob started college in 1960. Tommy was born soon after and Charlotte two years after him. Phil and Amelia were married in 1964, the spring before they graduated. During those four years, the four of them did almost everything together. Phil enlisted when he graduated, and was sent straight to Vietnam. Bob didn't enlist and wasn't drafted. Bob felt ashamed somehow. He wasn't a draft-dodging hippy, but he had to admit to himself that he was afraid. So he was all gung-ho about the war, but told people that the real reason he didn't go and fight was that his plant was working on some important top-secret chemical that would swing the battle for America. His research was vital and ultimately would save thousands of American lives.

Watching Amelia and Gordy now, made his guts twist up. He tried to convince himself that he was defending Phil's memory, but when he was very drunk and feeling reflective, he had to admit that he had been jealous of Phil. Phil was an all-round good guy that everybody liked. He was a star quarterback, probably good enough to make the pros. He had a great sense of humour, good grades at college and a pretty wife. It didn't matter that Gloria was just as pretty as Amelia. Bob knew that he wasn't as perfect as Phil. When Phil left amidst a big hero's farewell, Bob could hardly say goodbye. He was that racked with envy. When news came back, just a few months later, that Phil was missing in action, Bob felt responsible. He must have wished bad luck on him. He was desperate to blame somebody else.

Amelia was catatonic when she heard the news. She lost the baby she was carrying and started to change. She became withdrawn, not the flirtatious woman she used to be. The pounds started piling on. The once petite Amelia soon weighed 150 pounds, which settled heavily on her 5 foot 2 inch frame. Eventually June Thompson started dragging her to cocktail parties. She started to regain her coquettish nature and men found her even more attractive. There was something about the way she held herself, the way she rolled her large thighs as she walked. She was like one of those immense pink and white ladies ravaged by satyrs in museum paintings. Men fantasized about her.

But Amelia never really responded until she met Gordy. Most of the neighbours seemed to like the idea of Amelia and Gordy together.

'What are the chances of Phil being alive in the jungle?'

they would say. 'Hasn't she suffered enough? The poor woman deserves some happiness.'

Gordy kept protesting that Amelia shouldn't rush into anything. Phil could be a POW. 'What if he's released and comes home to find that Amelia has remarried?'

But no one really ever answered that question. They would shrug or mumble and hedge the question. Only Jack would say, 'Amelia can't spend the rest of her life worrying about the future. This is where we are now. Who knows where we're going? Let the woman have a little happiness.'

Gordy was sitting next to Amelia, showing the kids card tricks. Katie kept saying, 'How did you do that?'

Gordy would answer, 'A magician never gives away his secrets.' Amelia would laugh extra hard each time he said that, like it was some kind of private joke.

'Hey, Bob!' Rusty called out. 'Why don't you come have a beer with us? You've done your bit over there.'

'Yeah,' Lucy said. 'Let's just leave the coals until it's time for the marshmallows.'

Bob settled himself into the lawn chair Gloria had pulled up next to her.

'The hamburgers were just delicious, Bob,' she said.

'Thanks.'

Gloria tried to pat his hand, but Bob reached out and picked up his beer.

'What a cook you've got there!' Amelia said to Gloria.

Gloria retrieved her hand from the arm of Bob's chair and touched the edge of the smile she directed at Amelia.

'I wish Walter knew how to cook something,' June sighed. 'He can't even make toast without setting the bread on fire.'

'That's because you have such a supersonic, new-fangled toaster. Walter hasn't figured out how it works yet,' Jack chipped in.

'Watch out everyone. Toast time – duck and cover!' Gordy shouted before crouching into the nuclear-warning position.

Everybody laughed but June and Bob.

Bob took a long drink from his beer and wondered how he had ended up here. He couldn't remember ever deciding that this was where he wanted to live, this was the job he wanted to do, this was the family he wanted to have. I just need to have the same things as everybody else, he thought. And I just need to know that what is mine is *only* mine. I *need* to know that. That's what keeps me going.

'I don't see what's wrong with progress,' June complained. 'This is the *space* age, not the Stone Age! There are new things to have, new things to do. Science has really changed things – it's made a whole new world for us. A whole new universe. The space race means we have to lead the way or we'll be left behind. There will be nothing left for us to have.

'Just think of all those satellites up there,' she said, pointing at the darkening sky. 'They look just like stars. You can hardly tell the difference from down here. And we made them. They belong to us. I call that progress.'

They all leaned back in their lounge chairs and tilted their faces up. The sky was a deep purple and lit up with summer constellations and the tattoos of fireflies. The kids followed their trails of light and trapped the sparkling insects inside glass jars. They wove pieces of summer grass around their fingers like the wedding rings their parents wore. Then they would pull a firefly from the jar and tear out its stomach – a phosphorous gem for their eternity rings, shimmering pale green in the dying summer evening. A fragile light that mesmerized like the mysterious whirl of satellites.

On Flamingo Lake

Mrs Myrna Pepperidge was the local dance teacher and lived in a tiny bungalow by the edge of Flamingo Lake. Flamingo Lake had never been called anything more than 'Pepperidge Pond' or just 'the Pond' for all the years that Mrs Myrna Pepperidge had lived there and, for that matter, all the years that Old Man Pepperidge and his wife had lived there before Myrna became the only surviving Pepperidge. But all that changed when Myrna got an idea into her head to somehow make use of that useless pond – to make it shine and shimmer in the way lakes did in picture postcards or in those paintings by Monet.

Mrs Myrna Pepperidge had never married, but she felt 'Mrs' gave her more gravity and dignity as a dance teacher. She disliked the notion that people might think she was a dance teacher merely because she wasn't married and needed to make a living. Dance came first and foremost in Mrs Pepperidge's life and she made it plain that she would have been a dance teacher no matter what her marital circumstances were. She even took to wearing her mother's wedding ring as if it were her own and liked to think that she was a little like those Catholic nuns who believed they were married to Jesus. She never really understood how Jesus could have spread himself so thin, but she kind of liked the idea. Mrs Pepperidge used to twirl the ring on her finger and think, I'm married to the Muse – to the Muse of Dance, and I dedicate myself to all that is shining and wonderful and graceful, to all that is more beautiful than what we see in this mere world.

But Mrs Pepperidge was something of a contradiction: while dedicating herself to things higher than the world surrounding Pepperidge Pond, she also felt that things had to be useful or else they were a waste of space. All the objects in her home had an immediate and apparent function and she had only enough essentials to accommodate one person. She did keep a spare chair on hand, but it was not designed to encourage visitors to rest for long. Paintings were an exception to this rule. She felt they imbued her home with an atmosphere of culture, and that they also covered any startling irregularities in the paintwork. Mrs Pepperidge prided herself in seeing not only the cultural aspects of things, but also the practical side.

Dance was a prime example of this. Mrs Pepperidge would expound on the importance of dance during the September enrolment luncheon for students and parents, which she conducted by the side of Pepperidge Pond. She would clap her hands for everyone's attention, then begin to speak.

'Girls and boys, mothers and fathers, we are gathered here today in an informal manner, amidst the glories of late summer, before the shiver of autumn is upon us. And this, if you think about it, is a metaphor for life . . .' Mrs Pepperidge would pause significantly at this point every year, and with a graceful sweep of her arm indicate that the congregation were on the verge of something special. 'On our journey from summer to autumn, and finally to winter, what do we have to guide us? Do we have a path that is straight and well-defined that leads us through both the dangers and the beauties of the unknown? Perhaps, but perhaps not.' She would shake her head gently and look solemnly at each face, then speak again in a slightly more commanding voice. 'This is what I hope to give your children, to my pupils, to these students of dance.' Mrs Pepperidge would beckon all of the youngsters forward to a small semi-circle in front of their parents. 'By learning all the correct positions, steps and movements, through this grand discipline leading to beauty, you will discover a useful way to combine the physical and the spiritual – and will dance forward confidently through life.'

Then Mrs Pepperidge would gently raise both arms and lead the children through a *grand plié*. The crowd was always impressed by this elegant gesture and relieved and grateful to know that their children would dance through life in a more delicate way than they had.

Summer after summer, Mrs Pepperidge taught the local children how to dance by the edge of Pepperidge Pond. She did this for quite a few years and went on to teach the children's children. This fact began to weigh upon her mind and she finally grew restless and rather snappish with her pupils. 'Straighten up, Debbie!' she would say sharply, thumping the ground near the unlucky twelve-year-old's feet. 'You are hunched over like an ape. I have never seen anything quite so unattractive in my life.' Mrs Pepperidge would stalk to the front of the class again and, spine reinforced with steel, lead the class with angry vigour. 'First position! Second position! Come, now, dance! Elevate yourselves!' The covey of pink and black leotards would bob and wobble, ducklings scrambling without an ounce of grace by the edge of the pond.

Mrs Pepperidge watched this inelegant performance

three times a week, all through the summer of 1967 and started to lose faith in the Muse. All those years of teaching, all those years of bobbing and wobbling – Mrs Pepperidge felt that her life had not progressed, and that she wasn't bringing the soul of art any closer to her neighbours' lives. They did try, bless them, but year after year nothing changed, nothing shone, nothing glimmered.

Mrs Pepperidge was not quite sure what she should do. If you dedicate your life to the Muse, but the Muse lets you down, how should you react? What would those nuns do if Jesus dropped them like a hot potato and left them with a congregation of atheists? Mrs Pepperidge leafed through her jumbo-sized, full-colour plate art books until she found a good picture of the drowned Ophelia. She looked peaceful. Mrs Pepperidge took to practising Ophelia's position in the lake on the living-room floor.

Summer was drawing to a close and Mrs Pepperidge couldn't quite decide whether her body would float in a manner quite so elegant as that which she had managed to choreograph for the floor. She thought she would concentrate on the end of year performance for a while, then return to matters of life, destiny and her grand finale.

Mrs Pepperidge taught her students a short, simple piece to perform for the August afternoon set aside for their final show. She helped them make frothy costumes from pink and white tulle and showed them how to put on the little *diamanté* tiaras they bought from Mrs Lenzi's millinery shop. During the dress rehearsal, she prayed the next day would bring rain.

The night before the performance was not a good one for Mrs Pepperidge. The air was thick and heavy to the point of suffocation – heat lightning crackled through the sky, punctuated by drum rolls of thunder. A full moon glared sporadically through the window, voyeur to the peculiar shadows that skimmed and flickered across her walls. Mrs Pepperidge pulled the sheet up over her head and clutched it tight. She could hear strange noises and what she thought was laughter somewhere outside in the night.

Mrs Pepperidge was up as soon as it was light, glad the darkness was over. She made an extra strong pot of coffee and poured herself a large mug to drink out on the porch. The screen door banged shut behind her as she walked over to the porch swing. She swayed back and forth with her eyes closed, sipping her coffee. When she opened her eyes, the mug dropped, smashing on the floorboards of the porch. Mrs Pepperidge stared – first at the pond, then up towards Heaven. The Muse had presented her with a miracle, her own special miracle to commemorate all her years of unstinting faith. There, all around her pond, was a vision of that shining, shimmering place that the visionaries of this world occasionally glimpsed. The flamingoes had arrived – from somewhere. By magic, chance, a swooping down from space, but they were there. Close to a hundred flamingoes – pink and plastic and suitably durable, of the ordinary home and garden variety. They flocked by the edge of the pond, each balancing on one leg and listening for something in the early light of morning. Mrs Pepperidge did not question the Muse, but instead rushed to the edge of Pepperidge Pond and knelt to kiss its very shores.

'Flamingo Lake,' she cried. 'It shall be called Flamingo Lake.' Mrs Pepperidge returned to her house and began major preparations for her journey into town.

It was only two hours before the annual performance when Mrs Pepperidge returned from her shopping spree and dumped two large bags on to her front lawn. She arranged the flippers in an interesting pyramid shape near the edge of the lake. She lay snorkels and goggles in an intricate pattern around it. The girls and Tommy Jameson arrived at 11 a.m.

Mrs Pepperidge was more animated than they had ever seen her – and in a nice way for a change. She was all kind of sparkly and smiling; she told them exactly what they were going to do and said it like she thought they could really do it. The girls shook out their tulle skirts and put their tiaras in place. Tommy couldn't believe his luck – water, his element. He couldn't persuade his seven-year-old muscles to lift any of his fellow dancers in a fashion anywhere nearing elegance, but water might save the day. Now they wouldn't be able to make fun of his mother for having a clutsy son and the neighbours might talk to her. Mrs Pepperidge cleared her throat and the children all turned to look at her.

'Girls and boys – dancers . . . it will not be possible to properly rehearse the final show, but I'm sure you will be just fine.'

The kids looked at each other. Mrs Pepperidge seemed to think they could do it – this was a new one. They pulled the tulle skirts over the bathing suits their dance teacher had asked them to wear that morning and put on their flippers.

'All right, children, time to warm up while I prepare for our audience. First position, second position . . . ' Mrs Pepperidge continued to count out positions as she arranged a cluster of deckchairs around the edge of the pond. A few minutes later they heard the sound of car doors slamming and the parents trudging down to the chairs. 'Have a seat, ladies and gentlemen. The annual performance of this year's dancers will begin in five minutes.' Mrs Pepperidge bowed towards the parents and their deckchairs then returned to her dancers. 'Are you ready? Good. Take your positions and when the music begins, take to the water.'

'Yes, Mrs Pepperidge,' the children chorused.

Mrs Pepperidge hurried over to the porch and plugged her record player into the extension cord. She poised the needle over the record and called, 'One and a two and a three ... ' Strains of *Swan Lake* began to float over Pepperidge Pond. The children flip-flopped gracefully into the water. Their parents put down their complimentary glasses of ice-tea and began to clap loudly. The children swam their ballet beautifully, flippers flopping, tutus float-ing, tiaras in place. Tommy Jameson flipped the girls off his shoulders and swam with amazing grace. Mrs Pepperidge was a happy woman.

Mark Brown and the boys cycled up the road to the pond. 'Do you think anyone has noticed yet?' They all laughed and cycled faster. 'You know,' he said, 'I didn't think there were that many pink flamingoes in this town. I mean, Mrs Weatherby had twenty-five in that crazy garden of hers, but a hundred altogether!' He laughed. 'Guess we'll have to put them back. Do you think they'll know whose is whose?'

They pulled up to the end of Mrs Pepperidge's driveway and coasted to the back of the audience. 'Jeez,' muttered Mark, a little too loudly. 'What's going on?'

'My miracle, young man,' said Mrs Pepperidge. 'The miracle on Flamingo Lake.'

We've Gone Electric

Walter and June were the first couple in the neighbourhood to get an electric toothbrush set, and Rusty and Lucy were the first to get a divorce. These two events really set the neighbourhood talking and were more connected than they seemed.

In July 1960, just after their wedding, Walter and June bought a very nice salt-box house in a good neighbourhood in a place called Tinicum, not that far from Philadelphia. Walter could commute to the city in half an hour during the rush hour and, if he worked late, get home in twenty minutes.

That same summer Lucy and Rusty bought the house next door with the money Lucy inherited after her grandfather was run down by a motorcycle. Lucy was tempted to buy Rusty the biggest, most expensive bike she could find with the money – it seemed an appropriate gesture cantankerous Pops would have approved of. But when her inheritance was released to her on her eighteenth birthday, Lucy decided a house was probably a better idea.

So, the Thompsons and the Simons settled into Tinicum. Walter had two promotions during his first year working for a big advertising company and June started knitting.

When she and Lucy met up for their afternoon coffee and gossip, the conversation steered over to babies before too long.

'What do you think of these?' June held up a pair of yellow booties.

'Nice,' said Lucy. 'Hey, you got any cigarettes?'

'Nope,' June answered. 'I've given up. I don't think a mother-to-be should smoke. You need all the lung power you can get.'

'Oh.' Lucy worked her way through a pack on a good afternoon, a pack and half on a bad one. She would imitate various movie stars and the way they smoked, keeping June in stitches most of the time until she almost forgot about motherhood for a while.

'Who's this?' Lucy would say, rolling her hips or flicking a wrist or blowing smoke rings over her shoulder.

'Rita Hayworth' or 'Elizabeth Taylor' or 'Zsa Zsa Gabor' June would scream out, then grab the cigarette and do her own impression of Sophia Loren or Natalie Wood.

At least once a week, June would jump up in the middle of their coffee break and say, 'Hey, wait till I show you this!' She would gallop around the kitchen or into another room in the house and return to the table clutching some new kind of gadget. 'You have to get everything just right before you have a baby. Now, watch,' she would say and flick a switch. First it was an electric mixer, then a carving knife, then a can opener. 'Great, right?' June would smile. 'It saves lots of time. This,' she'd say, waving her newest electric appliance, 'is modern living.'

Every time June brought out a new gadget for Lucy to have a look at, Lucy got a funny sinking feeling in her stomach. At home, she thought about all the Thompsons' electric appliances whenever she went to open a tin of sweet corn or use her beat-up old vacuum cleaner. Lucy never mentioned June's gadgets to Rusty; she knew they couldn't afford time savers, that the time she saved wouldn't be worth the money they would have to spend to save it. But she couldn't help thinking – particularly when she found out that she was pregnant.

By this time June had already had Caroline and was a regular gold mine of advice. 'You need a lot of rest, Lucy,' she would admonish. 'You shouldn't spend all that time climbing ladders and moving furniture.' But Lucy couldn't help it. She had this urge to really fix up the place and Rusty helped out whenever he could. Now that he had his shop out in the garage in pretty good shape, Rusty started working at Mike's Garage part time and spent most of the rest of his waking hours working on motorcycles. Lucy didn't like to point out that he was actually bringing in less money for working more hours because he was always giving his friends these special deals. But the lack of cash was making things a little tough. And, to top it all off, the customers Rusty was keeping were not too popular with the rest of the neighbourhood. He was well known for being one of the best mechanics around – and for being something of a soft touch. He knew how to do tattoos and after a couple of beers on a Saturday night would practise inking a few guys, free of charge. The guys would bring their bikes over for all kinds of repairs and sometimes they would have a design on a piece of paper that they wanted Rusty to recreate onto some part of their body. For all of these favours, Lucy and Rusty would be allowed the honour of riding with the Warlocks every now and then. Everyone thought Rusty was a really good guy.

But the neighbours just couldn't get used to men wearing helmets with animal horns glued on to them roaring around the neighbourhood block. Lucy had always been something of a rebel, but she wasn't keen on being ostracized by all the neighbours. Sometimes, she thought, it's just easier to fit in.

Katie was born in August 1961 and Franky was born fourteen months later. Rusty had a lot more customers bringing bikes to the garage and had established a pretty big reputation as a tattoo artist, but it was pretty hard to make ends meet. June and Lucy were still the best of friends, but Lucy just couldn't help feeling a twinge of jealousy deep down in her stomach whenever June showed her some new prize. The Thompsons seemed to have everything.

Things didn't change much during the next few years either. The moment of terrible truth finally occurred in the early summer of 1967. After lunch one day, June brought out the electric toothbrush set. 'Pick a colour, any colour except for blue or yellow,' she instructed. Lucy selected the brush attachment with the green square on it. 'OK,' June said. She put the brush on to the electric toothbrush base, squeezed on a little toothpaste, then switched on. 'There you go,' she said triumphantly, handing the shivering brush to Lucy. 'Try it out.'

Lucy tentatively pushed the brush into her mouth and dribbled toothpaste all over herself as the toothbrush tickled her gums.

'It's the most modern development in dental hygiene,' June explained proudly. 'No more cavities!'

Lucy brooded over the electric toothbrush set for a couple of days. She wasn't exactly sure why they were better for your teeth, but she wanted one. She knew they couldn't afford gadgets, but the toothbrush set weighed on her mind. It was really the final thing in a whole line of electric conveniences that she knew she would have to do without. Lucy knew that 1967 was supposed to be the space age and things were supposed to be getting better all the time. But they were still struggling and the space-age dream of modern living where everything was done for you haunted her more and more. It was hard not fitting in when the rest of the neighbourhood was moving towards the future, and they seemed stuck in the slow lane with nothing but a good motorcycle and the makings of a tattoo parlour.

That next weekend, June asked Lucy and Rusty to keep an eye on the house for them as she, Walter and Caroline were going to the Poconos for a vacation.

'Just pop in when ever you like, Lucy,' June said, patting her on the arm. 'Take a load off your feet. Use whatever you want – the TV, the stereo, the blender. Have some rest and relaxation.'

So Lucy would go in once a day and check on everything. She would potter around and play a couple of records or borrow the blender to make some dessert or brush her teeth using the electric toothbrush. But one day she just couldn't stand it any more. There was just too much electricity around her. Lucy sat down in the reclining armchair and began to cry. There was no real reason, just a feeling that somewhere along the line she had failed, and that some- how she didn't know how she felt about anything these days.

When the tears stopped, Lucy got up and went into the kitchen. She turned on the mixer, the dishwasher, the wash- ing machine, then walked into the living room and flicked on the TV and the stereo. Lucy climbed the stairs, went into the bedroom and turned on all the lights, the radio, the electric blanket. In the bathroom she found Walter's electric razor and June's lady razor and left them humming, put the quivering toothbrush back in its holder and sat down on the lid of the toilet and listened.

Lucy listened for a very long time to the house buzzing and quivering, different pitches and vibrations shifting in layers all around her. She lay her head on the cool surface of the bathroom counter and felt the electricity humming through the house.

I've got to do something, she thought. It can't go on like this for ever.

She listened and could almost hear the telephone lines outside buzzing with voices, voices moving to and from the neighbourhood. Voices giving her some kind of answer she couldn't quite make out.

Mrs Weatherby's Garden

After Hank died, Greta Weatherby stayed drunk for ten days straight, then hitchhiked clear from New Orleans to Tinicum, Pennsylvania without sleeping a wink. It's only about a six-day drive if you take it real easy, but the road seemed to go on for ever with her watching every single mile go past. After ten days on the bottle, most people would want to sleep it off a little, but Greta couldn't do it. Her eyes would start dropping, then, like a pair of window shades, would roll right up every time they hit a bump or pothole in the road. And every time that happened she'd see this big bastard of a truck heading straight for them, rolling too fast down that hill, and she'd feel the swerve as Hank pulled the steering wheel hard to the right. Greta would see the flying glass and hear the noise, feel herself thrown clear, and see Hank slumped over the steering wheel – his heart giving out, the doctors said, before his neck was even broke.

So that was that. Another part of her life closed. All Greta could think to do was knock herself out for a while and hope that some great wish or dream or vision would emerge from the fog and give her an indication of what she ought to do. She had a lot of dreams in those ten days. But when she snapped out of them, Greta didn't recollect much and decided in the end that she ought to just get back home. Back home to the house left to her when her mother, then her grandparents, Jack and Tilda, died. To the old place in the middle of nowhere that she grew up in. So Greta started hitching.

Her Mother had died in 1958 and Grandma and Grandpa Hegarty just a short while after that. All of them from natural causes: if you call having a heart attack while sitting on the front porch, natural; falling off a stepladder while trying to put pickled cucumbers on the top shelf of the pantry, natural; or waking up dead when you're the only one left to even notice, natural. That March made for a lot of funerals for the Hegarty family. Hank and Greta spent more time than usual anchored in one place: Tinicum, her home town, was a place she hadn't set more than a couple of feet in for fifteen years. Then suddenly there she was, thirty-three years old and heading back to Tinicum for the second time in all those years. And this time it was to stay.

Now, normally Greta wouldn't have taken to hitchhiking on her own – not for that many miles anyway. But sometimes when you're not too sure about anything any more you do some crazy things. You just start walking around like you're in a dream and someone else is doing all your talking for you. Somebody puts your thumb out for you, someone opens the door, and someone gets you in that car or truck before you even know what's happening. Then you've got to make all the conversation and start wondering if maybe you ought to let it be someone else's life you're going to talk about during those miles. Kind of rewrite the past a little. So Greta would talk through those miles and be all sorts of people on the way, never really caring if something was going to happen. If someone pulled off the road and levelled a shotgun at her head, Greta probably wouldn't have even blinked.

Greta had some crazy rides with some crazy people, but maybe they weren't any more nuts than she was at that time. They would tell her all kinds of things: what they did for a living, what kind of music they liked, who they were in love with, who they were running from, all the things they were going to buy some day, and what they regretted most in their lives.

She had seen a lot of places in her fifteen years of travelling around the country and talked to a lot of people in the truckstops and diners on the road, but in a funny way she started matching up all the places she had seen with all the stories those people started telling her. It gave her something to think about besides Hank, and that stack of memories thumping at her like a bad hangover could be put to one side for a little while.

Then one day Greta was at the State line, crossing into Pennsylvania in the back of a big old '56 Buick. That tail-finned monster was painted aqua and had a white steering wheel with serrated edges to ease your fingers into plus a dashboard with all the latest gadgets of its day. George and Joe were in the front seat: George was driving and knocking back a bottle while Joe kept up a running commentary straight through the entire ride.

'Yeah, George here loves whiskey better than Peter loved God. I remember one day when he talked to this beautiful woman and she turned her nose up. I thought she was just being cute, poured myself a drink and started talking to her. And what do you think? Same response. Drinking's no good . . . It just makes you broke, sick, and ugly. I'm already ugly – I want something to make her better looking.' He told the same story a couple of times during that ride and every time he'd slap his leg and laugh and say, 'Well, guess

I'll just have one small swig. One small swig for the road.'

George and Joe decided to drive Greta all the way to Tinicum, though it was kind of out of their way. They shifted down Tinicum Pike and suddenly there was the old place, same as it had been for years. It was just that the world around it had changed since Greta was a child. Hundreds of those salt-box houses seemed to have sprung up like mushrooms around the place. All the farms were sold off and parcelled into quarter-acre plots with a Monopoly-board house stuck straight in the middle. The countryside and woods were gone except for the big old oaks on her land and those near the pond at the Pepperidge place about a mile across from all those new houses. Old Man McFarland's house and the post office were gone too. Yeah, Greta and Hank saw this kind of thing a lot when they were travelling. They went through the same small town maybe twice in two years and would really see how things had changed. The space age moving in: new houses, new cars, new gadgets – the emptiness disappearing bit by bit.

Hank and Greta had travelled through every State but Hawaii. They were planning a special trip there without the truck. And everywhere they went they took as many pictures as they could. Hank and Greta at Yellowstone Park. Hank near the Empire State Building. Greta on the beach in Escondido, California. Hank wearing a cowboy hat at a rodeo in Texas. Everywhere they went they made sure to go and see something when Hank wasn't working and to collect some little thing from that place. When the truck started getting too full of souvenirs, Greta would pack them in a sturdy box and have them sent on back to Tinicum to be put in the attic. Home for Hank and Greta was the truck and wherever they ended up by the end of the day. They liked it that way, always moving around, the two of them together just living nowhere in particular. The old house was a place to keep memories, road markers for where they'd been on their journeys.

George and Joe wouldn't come into the house for one last drink. When you travel with somebody and tell them all the crazy things you've thought about or done in your life, somehow you can't just stop and look at where they come from or how they live in an everyday way. That's just how it is with secrets and strangers. So they finished off one full bottle of whiskey while sitting in the driveway, laughing and telling stories. But when the last drop was drained, they drove off honking the horn and waving until Greta couldn't see the Buick any more. She went inside the old house and was at a loss. It seemed smaller than she remembered, but much emptier.

Greta got used to the place slowly, living out of a suitcase for over a month. Then one day she got it into her head to have a look through all the boxes in the attic. That's when Greta had her idea. She pinned a big colour map of the USA on the living-room wall and carried down all the boxes that were sorted and labelled by State. Starting with Alabama she emptied every box into separate piles on the living-room floor and by the time she got to Wyoming, clear into the dining room. Greta examined every single photograph and all the souvenirs they had collected. She made notes and drew diagrams in a thick leather-bound notebook she bought at the five and dime at the new shopping centre. It took over six months of planning, but when the first steady warm days of spring arrived, Greta was ready.

The garden shed had all the tools in it she needed plus bits of things Grandpa had thought he might find useful some day. Things like balls of string, old bottles, chickenwire, tin cans, newspapers, pieces of wood and odds and ends of junk, all stored neatly in cardboard boxes and labelled in his careful handwriting. Greta had a load of bricks and some bags of cement delivered and dumped next to the shed. She went to work.

It took her a while to get the hang of the cement and bricks, but soon Greta was building the kind of structures she had drawn in her book. The three-acre garden was carefully markered, small signs indicating where each State would be. Greta decided to work alphabetically and put a gold star on each State on her US map when she had completed that place.

Greta was up every morning at 5.30 and after a cup of coffee, started working. That first year took her through to C: Alabama, Alaska, Arkansas, Arizona, California, Colorado, and Connecticut. This was an interesting range of places and Greta was real pleased with how her work turned out. She had begun to build walls and patio areas throughout the garden. States were outlined in the cement and special souvenirs were embedded in the concrete.

Greta began constructing statues that represented the spirit of each place to her. Maybe an Indian warrior, a pack of wolves, a Civil War soldier, or big fish from the Pacific. They inhabited her garden, these creatures made from everyday things, held together with her memories and a thin crust of cement.

She knew the neighbours thought she was crazy, but her work gave her something to live for. All those memories stuck inside her head came tumbling out, straight through her fingers and into her garden. Slowly, everything she and Hank had done in the last fifteen years was starting to make sense. Hank and Greta had had a lot of fun together and so she was making this big pattern that traced out all they did. Like a huge 3-D picture book that didn't have a visible end.

Sometimes when the weather was too wet to get much accomplished, Greta thought about the plain white headstone with Hank's name on it. Just like the headstones that spelled out the names of her grandparents and mother. Those white slabs of marble made her sad. You could stand on the big, perfect green lawn looking at a white rock with someone's name on it, and you wouldn't be able to picture the person who was supposed to be underneath it. Sometimes Greta got real depressed when she looked at the rain as it ran down the window. Her garden took her away from all that.

As Greta worked on her garden she thought about all the places she had been to and remembered all the people she had met. She wondered what they were doing at that very minute and made up little stories about them. She worked those stories into her garden.

She also thought about her grandparents and her mother. All those years she was on the road, Greta never figured out why they'd never left Tinicum. Before she went on the road Tinicum was a tiny place in the middle of nowhere. The only people any of them really knew were each other. On those special nights when a farmer was too drunk to go home or a truckdriver pulled up for the night, it was a time for songs and storytelling. The world suddenly grew bigger without Greta even having to leave the front porch. Greta always wondered what kept her mother in Tinicum. Her beautiful mother who looked just like a movie star, and who all the truckdrivers used to whistle at. She just sat on the porch day after day, looking way out on to Tinicum Pike and swinging on the porch swing. Maybe Greta's father was one of those truckdrivers, and Eloise was waiting for him. Maybe her mother was a little crazy in the head. She had gone out on the road for her, looking in every State, trying to find some kind of answer.

But all that didn't really matter any more. Greta wasn't too sure, but maybe she did find her answer and it was busy resurrecting itself in her garden. She lived every day to a certain rhythm, the same old things happening over and over. She was never exactly sure what would appear like a dream and start building itself in her garden.

Maybe I live vicariously like my family did, Greta thought. They grabbed whatever memories they could from the strangers who landed up in Tinicum, Pennsylvania, population: six.

But maybe this time, I'm the person asking the stranger the questions, and the stranger with the memories is me.

Burning Like a Cigarette

Rusty lit a cigarette, then tilted his head back to have a look at the stars. They moved in a rush across the sky and made him dizzy. Rusty jumped hard and got the bike going. As he rode out of the neighbourhood, he could see Lucy's silhouette at the window, her cigarette flaring up as she took a drag on it.

The numbness made it hard for him to feel anything but the sides of his stomach pushing together. He tried to think back, to pinpoint when Lucy had stopped loving him. He couldn't find anything in his memory. He tried to think of the reasons. Maybe he spent too much time working on the bikes. Perhaps it was because when they were together they would just watch TV and not talk about anything all that exciting. He had never understood why a woman like Lucy would fall in love with a guy like him. Someone with no real education. Someone who would never be anything more than a mechanic. He had felt very lucky. Luck always runs out, he thought.

Rusty pushed the bike up over a hundred a couple of times, almost wishing something would happen. Maybe a deer would jump out from those scrubby Jersey pines or a drunk would come down the wrong side of the road . . .

anything to smack that numbness out of him. But there was nothing and his stomach just kept twisting round and round, no matter how fast he pushed the bike and how hard he tried not to think.

It had been very sudden. One night Rusty came in and washed his hands with detergent, as he usually did after working on a bike. Then he went to the fridge and got himself a beer. Lucy was sitting on the sofa watching an old movie on TV. He sat next to her and put his arm around her. Lucy didn't move, but he could feel her shoulder tightening up. They sat there like that for a while, the silence growing.

'Rusty,' Lucy had finally said. 'I think maybe we should call it a day.'

Rusty just sat there, a little bit stunned but not really all that surprised. He felt like a boxer gone down after one hard punch in the belly, just after the first round had started. It took Rusty a while to find the strength in his legs to get up.

'I'm just going to have a look at the kids, OK?'

'Rusty,' Lucy began.

'I think I need to take a ride.'

Lucy just looked at him, not knowing what to say.

Rusty went upstairs and opened the door to the kids' room. He walked in and bent down to have a good look at Katie and Franky. They were curled up with sleep in their own ways. Katie sprawled across her bed, one arm flung above her head and the other dangling down the side of the bed. Franky was curled in a ball, the covers pulled tight, almost over his head. Rusty shut his eyes to fix the picture in his brain, then leaned over and kissed them. They smelled of sleep and murmured little noises like birds.

*   *   *

Rusty looked at the darkness, the ghostly arches of pines looming over him, the sand on the side of the road. Then there it was. A new neon sign spelled out 'Honeymoon Motel', but everything else was still pretty much the same. It just had seven more years' worth of seediness about it.

Rusty went up to the front desk and rang the little bell. Ruby came out and he gave her a big smile. She looked at him with no trace of recognition. Rusty was a little disappointed that she didn't remember him. 'Hey, Ruby,' he said. 'How you doing?'

'Pretty good, kid, pretty good.' She looked at him expectantly for a couple of seconds while he waited for her to smile and say, 'Why, Rusty, Rusty Simon! How is that lovely wife of yours. Lucy isn't it?' But Ruby didn't say anything at all for a minute or so. She shuffled a few papers around before she spoke. 'Well, I guess you want a room.'

Rusty nodded silently, but blurted out as she started to hand him a key, 'Could you give me the honeymoon suite?'

'What?' she said. 'Honeymoons are for two, if you know what I mean. Someone waiting for you in the car?'

'I have a motorcycle,' he said.

'Oh.' Ruby gave him a hard look. 'Listen, fella,' she said. 'We run a clean place. And I don't like trouble. And I especially don't like smart-ass kids giving me a hard time at two in the morning.'

'I don't want to give you a hard time, Ruby,' Rusty answered. 'I just want to stay in the honeymoon suite. My wife and I stayed there seven years ago. After your husband married us.'

Ruby's face softened a little, but she kept her eyes locked on his.

'It had a great picture of Elvis on the wall.'

'OK, kid. But it's cash up front if you don't mind. I'm not the nostalgic type and I've got a business to run. You can have the honeymoon suite, but I'm not giving you any discount.'

Rusty walked into the room. He couldn't really remember exactly how the place had looked, but the picture of Elvis was still there. Yellowed from cigarette smoke and grime. Torn in a few places. But it was there. Rusty looked around the place, inspecting empty drawers, testing the shower for hot water, even seeing if the toilet flushed. There wasn't much to do after that. He got into bed and put a quarter into the box which started the bed vibrating. He lay there with the lights out, humming one Elvis song after another, until his quarters ran out.

Rusty woke up about 4 a.m. It was still dark, but enough moonlight came in the window so that he could see The King. Elvis seemed to be watching him and smiling this nice kind of smile. 'Elvis,' Rusty said to himself, 'Elvis would know what to do at a time like this. Elvis is a hero.'

Rusty got out of bed and got dressed. He walked outside and sat on the front step outside of his room. Elvis is out there somewhere, Rusty thought. Dressed up in white and gold like an angel looking down on the world.

Rusty lit a cigarette and took a long drag, trying to fill up the hole that was still aching in his stomach. He tilted his head back to have a look at the stars. Some things don't change, they just spin around in crazy patterns, but they don't really change. He lay back for a long time watching the stars. There were hundreds of them up there, bright as wishes, burning like his cigarette.

Playing Sally Starr

Katie buckled the holster around her waist, slid the white hat over her ponytail, and dusted off her boots. One last thing, the earrings. *Diamanté* and dangly – just like Sally Starr's. She twisted them on to her earlobes and admired the overall effect. Just like her. The earrings pinched, but she could live with it.

'OK, I'm ready. Let's have a look at you.' Katie inspected Franky's cowboy outfit: black boots, black hat, holster with the same shiny capguns as hers. 'Pretty good. You're the bad guy, I'm the good guy. You have to call me Sally and I'll call you – '

'The Lone Ranger?' Franky said, hopefully.

'Naw, he wore white. You have to be the bad guy. I can't think of a name right now. We'll just call you Frank until I think of something better.'

'Frank? But that's not – '

'Let's go,' Sally said. 'I'm the leader first. You can be later. Follow me.'

They stalked the prickle bushes, rolled under the split-rail fence, and made a break for the bushes near the front door. Sally pulled her gun out, cocked the trigger, carefully surveyed the scene.

'Coast looks clear.'

'Katie.'

'*Sally.*'

'Sally, do you really think we should do it?'

'You chicken or something?'

'No, but . . . '

'I thought you wanted to play cowboys?'

'Yeah, but . . . '

'Well, what's the matter with you then?'

'I don't want to get in trouble.'

'Cowboys don't care about getting into trouble. They just do things. Did a cowboy ever ask his mother first? Jeez! If he did that, he'd be dead at every shoot-out, right?'

'I guess. But the last time we—'

'Look, if you're going to be a scaredy cat about it, maybe you should just go home. Good thing I'm the leader. We'd never get anywhere following you around. Jeez, if you were Sally Starr, you wouldn't know what cartoon to show on TV. You wouldn't know anything, right?'

'I guess,' Franky muttered.

'Right. OK, here goes.'

Katie climbed up on to the windowsill of the picture window. She looked around again, gun poised. Lunchtime. Everyone must be inside eating sandwiches.

'You ready?' she stage-whispered.

Franky nodded.

Katie smashed in a pane of glass with her gun. She carefully broke all the jagged edges away with the gun, just like on TV. She climbed inside and unlocked the front door for Franky. They shut it and locked it again.

'Wow,' said Franky. 'It's so empty.'

They walked around the living room, footsteps echoing from carpetless floor to ceiling.

'Wow, it's empty. I've never seen an empty house before,' said Franky, softly.

'Yeah,' Katie agreed.

They explored further. They could see streams of dust floating as the sunlight charged through curtainless windows.

'I wonder if they left anything?' Katie said. They looked upstairs and downstairs, in cabinets and closets, hoping to discover a big treasure, but found only some stale bread and a couple of pennies.

'Hey!' Katie turned back to Franky. 'Let's go look at the basement.'

'The basement?'

'Yeah. That's where the party was. Maybe there's still balloons left or something. Remember all the stuff? Maybe there's even soda or potato chips left. I don't think everyone ate everything.'

'Maybe,' said Franky. 'Do you think the lights will still work?'

'Are cowboys afraid of the dark?' Katie rolled her eyes. 'Follow me.' They walked down the stairs to the basement. 'Hey!' Katie almost yelled. 'It's all still here!' They grabbed at the streamers. Franky threw a balloon and Katie shot it dead centre with her capgun. The showdown started.

Caps sparking, dodging fire, they made a break for the stairs. The fight continued through the kitchen, then upstairs into the parent bedroom. Katie kicked Franky. Franky knocked her hat off. Katie hit Franky on the arm. Franky grabbed Katie's hat up off the floor. They ran in circles around the room. Franky opened the closet door and threw the hat – it managed to reach the top shelf. Franky ran downstairs, then towards the basement and escaped through the back door. Katie chased after, but heard a noise at the front door. She stopped. The doorknob was turning. She ran back to the parent bedroom and shut herself in the closet. She held her breath.

Feet clumped up the stairs. Katie could hear Mr Gardner's voice.

'It's a very nice house,' Mr Gardner said. 'The perfect size. Two bedrooms. Just right if you want to have children.'

The couple nodded and smiled at each other. Mr Gardner was the real-estate agent and he lived across the street. He was Martha's father – and Cindy's and Georgie's too. Katie played with Martha sometimes, but no one else did much. Martha was retarded. The mothers in the neighbourhood were afraid that their kids would pick up bad habits and told them to stay away from Martha. Georgie was retarded too, but he wasn't very nice. He used to fight a lot. He'd hit anyone. He once tried to stab a teacher with some scissors. Luckily they were those funny left handed ones with green rubber handles. He couldn't work them right and didn't hurt anyone much.

'Children, have them while you're young,' said Mr Gardner. 'Nice to have them while you're young. We had them kind of late. We don't regret it, you know. But it's good to enjoy them while you're young.' The couple looked at each other and smiled. 'Yes, a lovely house for a new family,' Mr Gardner advised. 'A beautiful living room and kitchen. And look here! A nice view of the backyard.' They looked. 'This is the master bedroom. Very spacious, with its own private bathroom.' They clicked on the bathroom light and admired the fixtures.

'Honey don't you think the bed would look good about here?' She gestured coyly towards the corner, furthest from the baby's room.

'Yes, honey.' They prowled around some more. Katie held her breath for another twenty seconds, then softly took another gulp, shut her eyes and waited for them to leave.

'And closet space. Good closet space,' enthused Mr Gardner. 'Have a look. Lots of space.' The door opened. Three big shadows loomed over Katie.

'Hi,' she said. 'Could you get my cowgirl hat for me? I can't reach it.'

The man's jaw slowly worked its way open, but no sound came out. He reached up, then handed her the hat. She waited for them to yell, but the man, woman and Mr Gardner just stood there quietly, looking kind of surprised. Katie edged her way towards the bedroom door, trying to think of something to say so she wouldn't get into trouble.

'We found some old bread in a drawer in the kitchen,' Katie blurted out. 'Some ducks live on Mrs Pepperidge's pond. If you want to feed the ducks, there's some bread in the kitchen drawer. And if you have kids,' she said, 'they can keep bread there to feed the ducks.'

'Thank you,' the young couple said at the same time, 'thank you very much.' They secretly wondered if this neighbourhood really was a family neighbourhood, and if kids like this would be a good influence on their children.

'Thank you, Mr Gardner,' they said. 'We'll think about it. We'll think about it very hard.'

Katie hurried downstairs, then into the basement and out the back door while they were thinking and Mr Gardner was talking.

'Well, it was a real pleasure to meet you folks and I hope we'll be neighbours. I think you'll find that this is a family neighbourhood. Here in Tinicum, the people are the place – and this is a great place for kids to grow up in.'

The Satellite Lounge

The crackle from the clock radio woke her immediately. With a well-practised aim, Gloria hit the snooze button before the noise could disturb Bob. She lay on her side, watching the second hand circle, wondering why their radio always came untuned during the night. Gloria imagined airwaves stretching from the glowing green lines on their radio right up into space and the music sliding down those lines straight into the radio. Their airwaves seemed to wobble in the night so that their music was out of tune first thing in the morning.

Gloria folded the blankets back and eased her legs out of bed. She made her way into the bathroom, quietly closed the door before switching on the light, then listened – Bob was still snoring. Gloria stared in the mirror; her eyes were puffy and a crease ran across her cheek where it had been pressed into the pillow, but she thought she looked all right. After massaging cold cream into her face, she swished the make-up down the drain with a few splashes of cold water. Gloria inspected herself again after re-doing her face, then drew a white, filmy dressing gown over her négligé before making her way quietly to the kitchen.

The kitchen clock indicated 8 a.m. The kids were bound to wake up any minute and their noise would start Bob off in a bad mood. Gloria broke half a dozen eggs into a large tupperware bowl and laid a dozen strips of bacon on to some paper towels. After placing four plastic mats on the table, Gloria neatly arranged the dishes and cutlery. In a moment of inspiration she stood a small jar of flowers next to the orange juice and bottle of milk. She was whisking the eggs as Tommy and Charlotte came screaming into the kitchen.

'Shhhh! You'll wake your father!' They scraped back the kitchen chairs and started shaking cereal into their bowls. Gloria poured the eggs into the frying pan and put the bacon under the grill just as Bob grumbled into the kitchen and sat down.

'Coffee?'

He pushed his cup towards the pot in answer. Gloria poured the coffee, then put some hot buttered toast on the little side dish near his plate. She served Bob some eggs and bacon before sitting down. The kids left the remainder of their cereal in a sea of milk and sugar and raced off to the television.

Bob poured himself some more coffee and Gloria handed him the milk. He avoided touching her fingers when he took it. Bob ate his breakfast methodically while Gloria bit patterns in her toast, then left it.

'Are you playing golf today?'

Bob finished chewing and looked at her for the first time that morning. 'Ummm – with Jack and Walter. Tee-off at two o'clock.'

'That should be fun.' Gloria smiled, then took a sip of her coffee. She didn't know what else to say. They sat quietly for a few minutes. 'Would you like hamburgers or meatloaf for dinner?' she asked suddenly.

Bob thought about it for a few minutes before answering, 'Meatloaf.'

After dinner, Gloria scraped the dishes into the sink, then flicked on the garbage disposal. She stared out of the window as the disposal growled and chewed. When it was finished, she rinsed the dishes and put them into the dishwasher. Gloria pulled the yellow rubber gloves off and left them neatly by the sink. She put the leftover meatloaf in the refrigerator.

Bob was watching TV. She lingered hesitantly, but Bob stayed sprawled across the sofa and wouldn't turn his head to look at her. Gloria walked into the bathroom, had a quick shower, then began to re-apply her make-up. She examined her face and body carefully. She didn't think she looked so bad. Gloria dusted herself with powder.

Gloria pulled open her closet and looked at the dresses hanging neatly inside. She pulled out a pink one and held it in front of her. The reflection in the full-length mirror looked back, a question on its face. She decided to wear the gold dress with the spaghetti straps and her little diamond necklace and earrings. She put on the gold shoes with the bows, collected her handbag and the car keys before she clicked out the front door. Bob's eyes flicked once as the door snapped shut.

Gloria pulled into the parking lot of the Satellite Lounge, checked her face in the rear view mirror, then lit a cigarette with the dashboard lighter. She practised inhaling a few times, then got out of the car.

Gloria stepped into the lounge and looked around nervously. She saw June and Walter Thompson from around the block, who met her eyes but looked quickly away. They leaned towards each other to talk. Gloria made her way to the bar, hiked herself on to a bar stool and smiled at Jim.

'The usual, Gloria?'

'Thanks, Jim.' She stubbed out her cigarette and quickly lit another one. Jim placed a Martini in front of her.

'You want some peanuts, Gloria?'

She smiled. 'No thanks, Jim.'

'Go ahead. On the house. You're looking a little thin.' She laughed and sipped some of her Martini.

it was nine o'clock. The man in the nice suit had been watching her for quite some time. He sent another drink her way and Gloria smiled thank you. He moved to the bar stool next to her.

'Swanson. Bob Swanson.' He extended his hand. She shook it and smiled.

'Gloria,' she said. 'My name is Gloria.'

'Well, Gloria,' said Bob. 'I guess we were destined to meet. Between the two of us, we're somebody famous, right? Gloria and Swanson, now I call that destiny.'

They both laughed.

'Well, you'll never guess,' said Gloria. 'Just guess what my husband's name is?' Bob looked at her, unsure for a second. 'Why, Bob,' laughed Gloria. 'It's Bob, too. This must be fate.' They both laughed some more, clinked glasses and had another drink.

'May I have this dance, Gloria?' Bob stood up and with a sweep of his arm indicated the dancefloor.

'Why, thank you, Bob.' Gloria took his arm and they stepped under the coloured lights. They danced through four numbers until little beads of sweat were gathering on Bob's upper lip. Gloria could feel the dampness on her neck and the moisture of his left palm on her shoulder blade.

'That takes it out of you, doesn't it, Gloria? Shall we have another drink?'

'Thank you, Bob. I could sure use a drink.' Gloria fanned her face and laughed. They had two more Martinis.

It was 2 a.m. and Bob swore softly as he tried to unlock the hotel door. As the door swung open, Bob turned to Gloria and said, 'Allow me.' He picked her up, carried her into the room and put her right down on the bed. 'Thank you, Bob,' was all Gloria could think to say.

Bob carefully slipped off Gloria's dress and laid it across the chair. He unclipped her garter belt and eased her stockings gently down her legs, then unhooked her bra and drew it away from her breasts. She stared at the wall as she felt him slide her panties away.

'You're very beautiful,' he said over and over as he kissed her.

Gloria watched him, eyes half closed and thought that this room was not so different from their own. She remembered how at first everything had been all right. She remembered how, bit by bit, Bob curled further away, touched her less, flinched when she reached to touch him. She thought of how she started dressing up for bed: the make-up, the perfume, all the different nightgowns. Gloria closed her eyes. No, this room was not so different from their own.

The clock radio went off at 7 a.m., just like she'd asked. Gloria opened her eyes and looked at Bob. He was breathing heavily, face half buried in the pillow. She looked at the lines on his face, his thinning hair, his sagging belly. She watched him a while, not minding how he sprawled, tired and crumpled in the bed. She lay still a little longer, wondering why the music slipped from this radio into this room so perfectly, wondering how it fell without interference straight down from space.

The Fun House

At night the faces came. They circled his bed in a big arc looking at him, staring from the shadows. Franky pulled the covers up over his head, but the faces kept coming. They whispered to him through the night. Whenever he looked out into the dark, there they were floating down from the attic like circus balloons.

When he just couldn't stand it any more, Franky would escape from his bed and sneak quietly into Lucy and Vince's bedroom. He would curl up between them and fall asleep, comforted by Vince's snoring and the way Lucy would pull her arm around him even when she was asleep.

In the morning Vince would wake up and start complaining. 'What is this?' he would shout at Lucy. 'Can't you train your kids?' Lucy never really had an answer to that.

Franky wasn't very sure when the faces had started coming. All he knew was that the darkness called up uneasy feelings in him and terrible things were stirring within it.

But he did remember very clearly the day of the surprise trip to Willow Grove Park. It was August 4, Katie's eighth birthday and Vince had been living with them for three months. Katie and Franky didn't pay much attention to Vince. They didn't think he'd be there for ever. After all, their dad had moved to Florida – just like that. One day he was there, and the next he wasn't. With Vince it was the other way around. One day it was just the three of them, then one morning Vince was there for breakfast. And he stayed.

On Katie's birthday, Vince decided to impress everyone with a trip to what he said was the best amusement park in the USA. He gave Katie and Franky some change to buy cotton candy and soda, plus $2 to spend on rides. It was when they were walking over to the big roller coaster that Franky saw them. The faces were big and they didn't look right. Some had red skin with bumps and others very long teeth, and some had horns. These creatures were tall and their long arms stretched down towards the ground.

Katie said, 'Stand next to me and pretend to be scared.' Franky didn't need to pretend. The face he pulled while Lucy took the photo was more real than acted out. Franky was never sure whether the dreams came first or if seeing the space creatures in Willow Grove Park had started the nightmares.

When they reached the roller coaster, Katie turned to him and said, 'This is the biggest roller coaster in the country. Maybe the world. And the fastest. I don't think you're big enough to go on it. You're only six, and too short and too scared.' Franky couldn't argue with her. When they measured him against the line, he stood a couple of inches short of being allowed on the ride. 'See, I told you,' Katie said. 'You're a shrimp. You failed the height test. You're going to miss a really good ride.'

'Don't worry,' Lucy said quickly. 'Vince will take you into the Fun House and I'll go on the roller coaster with Katie. I'll bet the Fun House is just as good.'

'I'll bet it's not,' Katie piped up before Lucy could drag her on to the ride.

Vince moved off towards the Fun House and Franky trotted after him. They didn't have much to say to each other and Franky was glad when they were finally inside.

The Fun House was dark, and strange luminous shapes decorated the walls. Suddenly the floor tilted and Franky squealed with fear. A door in the wall flew open and a witch with a green face came screaming out. Then a coffin opened and a skeleton sat up and started laughing. Franky was feeling pretty scared. He couldn't understand what was supposed to be fun about this place.

They continued to shuffle down the eerie corridors and one gruesome creature after another popped out at them. Then a cold wind whooshed through the place and an ear-piercing screech came from a corner right near Franky. He squealed again, then reached up and grabbed Vince's hand. He wasn't sure Vince would like this much, but Franky was too frightened to care. He held on tightly as they continued through the rest of the Fun House.

When they reached the end of one corridor, suddenly the wall slid away and there they were back out in the daylight. Franky looked up and realized that it wasn't Vince's hand he was holding. 'Hey!' shouted Franky. 'You're not my daddy!' Franky was so panicked, he forgot who he was supposed to be with. The man smiled at him, but Franky wrenched his hand away and went running across the park. 'You're not my daddy,' he kept mumbling to himself as he ran.

Franky went looking for Vince and Lucy. He thought he could see the man following him. He ran as fast as he could, thinking the man was probably a murderer or something – something not very good. Franky pushed through crowds of people, but he kept spotting the man's face every once in a while. He was coming after Franky, with a strange smile on his face. Franky knew something terrible would happen if the man caught up with him, so he ran until he was tired and completely lost. He asked a woman at a cotton candy stand if she knew where the biggest roller coaster in the world was.

'Are you lost, honey?' she asked.

'I guess so,' he answered. 'I'm looking for my mommy and a man is chasing me.'

'A man? Why?' A look of suspicion crossed her face and crept into her voice. 'Did you take something?'

'No,' Franky answered. 'He was pretending to be my daddy.'

The woman looked alarmed and said, 'Come with me. We'll find your mommy for you.' She took Franky by the hand and they walked over to a small tent. 'This little boy is lost,' she said to the woman inside the tent. 'He needs to find his mother.'

'What's your name, honey?' the woman inside the little tent asked him.

'Franky,' he said.

'Franky what?'

'Franky Simon.'

The woman started calling his name over the loud-speaker. 'We have a little boy here who has lost his mother. His name is Franky Simon. He's waiting at the lost children tent. Will Franky Simon's mother come to the lost children's tent, please.'

Lucy got there pretty quickly, dragging Katie after her. 'We were just lining up to go on the roller coaster for the fourth time,' Katie said as soon as she saw Franky, 'and then we heard your name coming out of the loudspeaker. I'll bet you got lost on purpose just so that you could hear your name all over the place.'

All of a sudden Vince came striding up to them. 'What happened to you?' he asked Franky. 'You went running out of the Fun House like one of those glowing skeletons was chasing after you.'

'Scaredy cat!' Katie chimed in.

Franky just stood there, tired of all the noise, flashing lights and bright colours. 'I want to go home,' he said.

Before Katie could get a word in, Lucy took Franky by the hand and said, 'Me too. I'm getting pretty tired.'

That night he saw the faces circling his bed. He pulled the covers over his head, but they kept him awake all night.

The faces kept coming, they didn't look like anybody special – maybe just the man next door. Or the man with the strange smile. Or maybe one of the space monsters from Willow Grove Park. It didn't matter which, Franky knew that they were trying to get him.

Dreaming . . .

Lucy pushes the accelerator impatiently and the Mustang growls, chokes on a gear, then slips up to 80 m.p.h.

She watches both mirrors carefully, first the rear view, then the wing mirror and back again. There it is – a dazzle of red fender sneaking over the yellow lane, judging the time and distance.

Lucy looks around her. The road is choked with bad-tempered businessmen taking their families to the shore for a long weekend. She circles to pass a blue station wagon overloaded with suitcases, beach rafts and children screaming out the back window. The man driving has a heavy five o'clock shadow and dark eyebrows that work up and down with anger.

Lucy tries to edge past him, but he steps on it, refusing to let her cut back in lane. He zigzags in front of her. Her eyes search the mirror and she sees a red fender nosing forward, only one car away.

She skids, swerving the corner of the turnpike too wide. Her fingers pull at the wheel, the car fishtails. Gravel flies and shatters the wing mirror into a blindness of tiny pieces.

III

Lost in Space

What's good for General Motors is good for America.
  – Charles Erwin Wilson, President of General Motors
  Corporation

I defy any man to show me that there is pauperism in the United
States.
  – Andrew Carnegie

It is the unvarying law that the wealth of the community will be in
the hands of the few ... The great majority of men are unwilling
to endure that long self-denial and saving which makes accumulations
possible ... and hence it always has been, and until human nature
is remodelled always will be true, that the wealth of a nation is in
the hands of a few, while the many subsist upon the proceeds of their
daily toil.
  – Supreme Court Justice David J. Brewer, 1893

Our houses are all only one level, like our class structure.
  – *House Beautiful*, 1953

Bunnies or Rabbits

You run across some strange people when working nights in a hotel, and the hotel Cheryl Anne Simms worked in had their share of oddballs. Maybe it was the sign that attracted them: 'Bunnies or Rabbits, Pets or Meat'.

The sign was the first glimpse of civilization when driving down route 611 through the pine forests that covered the hills of North Carolina. It wasn't until about a mile later that another sign came into view: 'Hushpuppy Hotel, best home cooking for miles around' with a picture of a bunny painted in the corner and the words 'home-grown' underneath it. The Hushpuppy Hotel was known for the freshest rabbit stew ever tasted.

The Hushpuppy Hotel was a family concern and it had been doing business for over thirty years. It started out as a roadside diner during the Depression and turned into a hotel/motel for all kinds of people driving to or from something. Yeah, when you work nights in a hotel, you meet some pretty strange people. You can tell that from the way they look at you, the kind of vehicles they drive, or the things they leave behind in their room. The stuff people carry around when they're travelling tells a lot of big stories about them.

Cheryl Anne could remember a weekend in particular that was strange from the word go. One Friday night in late August she was working the graveyard shift and was feeling that usual mixture of tired and mean. It must have been 5 a.m. when a blonde woman and her two kids drove in. Cheryl Anne gave her the keys to room 19.

'Do you have any food?' the woman asked.

'We don't do room service, honey,' Cheryl Anne replied.

'What about some sandwiches or candy bars from the souvenir shop? My kids haven't eaten since lunch.'

'You must have left wherever you were in a real big hurry.' Cheryl Anne took a drag on her cigarette and stood looking at the blonde woman, waiting to see if she was going to try and explain why she was wearing babydoll pyjamas underneath a pink see-through raincoat.

The woman pulled her coat a little tighter and said, 'Yeah, we were in a rush. Now how about those sandwiches? Or some potato chips or something?'

Cheryl Anne flicked on the light at the end of the counter, but left the red neon 'Hushpuppy Hotel Souvenirs' sign off in case anyone else walked in and got any ideas about a special memento. She found three cheese sandwiches and a box of oreo cookies. 'That will be $3,' Cheryl Anne announced.

'Three dollars?' The woman flicked her eyebrows upwards in amazement.

'You're talking five in the morning, honey,' Cheryl Anne explained. 'The souvenir shop isn't usually open at this hour. I'm doing you a big favour.' Cheryl Anne handed the woman the food and took the money.

'Is this Florida, Mommy?' the little boy wondered.

'North Carolina, sweetheart,' she answered.

'Where are you all going?' Cheryl Anne couldn't help asking.

'Florida – to see our daddy,' the little girl mumbled while pulling up her pyjamas.

Cheryl Anne looked at them. Two kids in pyjamas with a woman in babydolls and a pink plastic raincoat and slippers. 'Bet he'll be glad to see you,' she said, her voice laced with sarcasm. 'Well, if you're checking out tomorrow, I need the keys before noon.'

'Before you close the shop,' the blonde woman said, 'can I buy a couple of T-shirts and some bermudas or something?'

'Well, if you have the money, why not, sugar?' Cheryl Anne pulled out three 'Good Home Cooking at Hushpuppy Hotel' T-shirts. 'Do you like the pink plaid or the green plaid bermudas?'

She took the green ones and a pair of sunglasses, and then wandered off to room 19 with her kids.

Lord, thought Cheryl Anne. You get all kinds when you work in a hotel.

Cheryl Anne was just starting the Sunday morning clean-up shift when she noticed the prettiest car she had ever seen sitting there in the parking lot. It was this shiny red convertible with a white interior. Something else. She had definitely never seen anything like it. North Carolina is a funny place when it comes to cars. The weather is so mild that cars just last and last. Most people Cheryl Anne knew drove a car or truck that was at least ten years old, maybe twenty. But this little number looked new, and Cheryl Anne was just dying to find out who had rolled up in it.

Her cousin Earl was setting up the souvenir shop as she walked in. 'Hey there, Earl,' Cheryl Anne shouted, watching his big belly strain against the tiny buttons on his white shirt. 'You've got to cut down on those beers, you know?'

'Yeah, yeah, Cheryl Anne. Always trying to do me out of the good things in life.'

'Earl,' she asked, 'whose red convertible is that out there?'

'I haven't seen any red convertible.' Earl walked to the door and peered out. 'Hey!' He raised his eyebrows and nodded to Cheryl Anne. 'Not bad. Wouldn't mind one of those myself.'

'Yeah, well,' Cheryl Anne said impatiently. 'Whose is it?'

'Beats me,' he shrugged and strolled back behind the counter.

Cheryl Anne went to check on the rabbits before cleaning up the vacant rooms. They had pens full of maybe thirty big fluffy rabbits at any given time. Nice rabbits – great for pets, even better for dinner.

Rabbit stew was a speciality of the house. Cheryl Anne's mother had made it for years and her sister Rosilee took over most of the cooking after their mother died. That's what the Hushpuppy Hotel was most known for: good home-style cooking after hours of travelling either north or south on the highway. The rooms were OK but their set-up was really more like a motel, though Hushpuppy Hotel had more of a ring to it. Their place was a family concern, started up by her father and his brother Jed, thirty years ago. The Simms had the only place for miles near the highway and probably the best food in the whole State.

Cheryl Anne checked the rabbits and decided that if no one drove up and asked to buy Rupert, he was heading for the stew pot. 'Raising rabbits is a lot like life in general,' Cheryl Anne always said. 'You shouldn't get too sentimental about any one rabbit or you'll be too soft to get it into the stew pot. And then you'll go hungry all because you liked the look of a bunny.'

So she left Rupert with a reprieve until the three o'clock dinner preparations and went into room 17. Cheryl Anne was starting to get the bed linen ready for the next people to roll in when she saw this man lying on the bed. On a bed he hadn't paid for. Then she put two and two together – this was probably the guy who drove up in the convertible. She stood there for a minute, looking at him. He was a good-looking guy and she could just picture him at the wheel of that car. She cleaned up the room a little, watching to see if he would wake up. Cheryl Anne was kind of hoping all the while he would, and he did. He near enough jumped out of his skin, but she just smiled and said, 'Sleep well? I'm just cleaning the place up a little. Are you staying another night?'

It took him a few seconds to get his wits together before he said, 'Uh, well, I really need to get a move on it. I have a tight schedule. I'm trying to find a friend of mine.'

'Oh, yeah?' Cheryl Anne asked innocently. 'Someone from around here?'

'No,' he answered. 'She's on the road. Maybe you've seen her? A blonde woman with two kids and a beat-up old Mustang.'

Cheryl Anne thought hard for about a minute, humming and hahing like she was trying to remember. Now, she didn't owe that blonde woman anything and Cheryl Anne was not what you would call a charitable person. But there's a certain pleasure to be got from watching a naked man squirm under a set of sheets he's not supposed to be in. Cheryl Anne wanted to make that moment last for a mighty long time. 'No,' she said in the end, 'I don't recollect seeing anyone like that around here. Not in quite a while anyway.' She watched him real careful to see how he would react to that, but the only sign of anger he gave away was his knuckles closing tight around the hotel room sheets.

'Well,' Cheryl Anne picked up a pile of rubbish and walked towards the door, 'will I be seeing you at supper?'

'What time is that at?' He relaxed back against the pillows

real casual, thinking that she didn't know he had broke into room 17.

'Six o'clock sharp,' Cheryl Anne told him. 'It's our special today,' she added. 'Rabbit stew. Fresh, home-grown and a recipe that goes back a lot of generations.'

'That sounds great. I'm Vince, by the way.' He gave Cheryl Anne a big smile. 'I'll see you at dinner.'

'OK, Vince. See you there.' Cheryl Anne winked at him as she closed the door behind her.

Cheryl Anne carried the Acme bag full of old food wrappers over to the dump and tipped it upside down. The stuff fell out in a heap and she noticed in all the old wrappers a full pack of Twinkies. When she went to fish them out for cousin Earl she noticed something else lying in the trash. A gun. Cheryl Anne picked it up, then checked to see if it was loaded. It was. She stood there thinking for a minute, feeling kind of sorry for the blonde woman and her kids. That woman sure knew how to pick them.

Then Cheryl Anne started thinking about a lot of things as she walked over to the rabbit pens. She thought about Jim and the time she caught him kissing that Suggs girl right under the pine tree that marked the west corner of their land. She remembered the time Tad Briggs knocked her over into the grass and kept pushing it into her no matter how hard she bit his arm. She remembered a lot of things that put her in a pretty damned bad mood. Cheryl Anne walked over to Rupert, held him by his ears at arm's length and shot him once straight through the head.

Dinner was good as usual and Vince sang its praises louder than anyone. 'Never ate rabbit before,' he enthused about a dozen times. 'Real nice.' He ate hearty, praising Rosilee and flirting at Cheryl Anne with his big, dark eyes. She just sat there watching him, laughing inside.

After Vince finished his big piece of apple pie, Cheryl Anne invited him for a stroll around the place. He was real complimentary and talked a blue streak, confident that he had got away without paying for a night's lodging and a good meal. He seemed to think that he had another free bed and probably Cheryl Anne's company in store for that night. Vince and Cheryl Anne were looking at the rabbits when he leaned over and kissed her. Cheryl Anne had to confess, she did feel a little bit of a twinge, but, Well, hey, she thought, you can't spend your whole life getting senti-mental about any one rabbit.

He whispered in her ear, 'You're one beautiful woman. Do you know that?'

'Why, thank you, Vince,' she said real genuine. 'I hope you enjoyed your stay.' Then she pulled the gun from behind the rabbit pen and shot Vince straight through the head.

In a small place in the middle of nowhere, populated mainly by people you are related to, you learn real quick that the law is a flexible thing. All in all, the law is exactly what you say it is. Cheryl Anne wasn't worried about any kind of retaliation from outsiders or from the law. Vince was a thief. He hadn't paid his bill and was trying to cheat good honest folk out of a living. He got everything he deserved.

Cheryl Anne had a lot of good times riding around in that beautiful red convertible. When you're driving down a road, with the pine trees arching over your head, the sun making gold patterns that flash like fish over the road, you get to thinking. You think about the feeling of the wind blowing your hair around and how one small push of your foot makes a good car like ɩ go over 80 miles an hour.

You think, but you don't get sentimental – you can't be soft if you want to survive. You just drive and think and remember. Yeah, it's funny how when you have a gun in your hand, sometimes you just have to pull that trigger.

Just Like on TV

He pulled one white sock up, then the other before pushing his feet into a pair of black loafers. Bobby Silverelli walked over to the mirror and inspected his hair. Slicked back, just right. He moved back a step, struck a pose and crashed a few chords on an imaginary guitar. Bobby studied his reflection critically, then dipped one knee further towards the floor.

Billy walked into the room and flopped on the bed. 'Well?' he asked.

'Well, what?' Bobby said to the mirror.

'It's almost time to go. Are you ready yet? You've been practising in front of that mirror and changing clothes for the last three hours.'

'This is a once in a lifetime chance, Billy. At least one of us is preparing for our future. Or do you want to be stocking shelves at the local Acme for the rest of *your* life? 'Cause I'm getting *out*.'

'Come on, Bobby. It's just one show.'

'It's one *chance*. People don't get two.'

'Awww, man . . . Look, I'm going to put the stuff in the car.'

'Keep the suit clean,' Bobby advised.

'If you'd give me a hand, that wouldn't be a problem,' Billy shouted back.

Bobby turned back to his reflection and did a big wobble as he played guitar and sang:

Man on the run!
Man with a gun!
Yeah, I'm on the run,
And I've got a gun ...

Bobby dusted down his pale blue suit, then went over to his handkerchief drawer and pulled out the rabbit foot he'd had since he was nine. He rubbed the foot three times whispering, 'Success, success, rise to the test and gain success.' Bobby put the foot in his pocket, spun around three times with his eyes closed, then hurried from his bedroom.

'This is it,' he muttered to himself as he ran down the stairs and out the front door.

This was the night. TV sets flicked on all over Tinicum and were tuned in to the 'Ed Sullivan Show'. Lucy, Katie and Franky sat clustered around their television, a bowl of potato chips and three bottles of Coke in front of them on the coffee table.

Ed Sullivan came out and told everyone that he had some very special guests that evening. 'Remember those boys from England – The Beatles? Well, I've got an even bigger treat for you tonight. Two all-American boys, twins in fact, singing a song they wrote themselves. And it's a true story ... Let me introduce to you, Bobby and Billy Silverelli!'

A curtain drew back and there they were, with their Buddy Holly glasses and Elvis Presley hairstyles. They wore matching pale blue suits and black loafers. Bobby had an electric guitar slung from a strap around his shoulder and

Billy stood behind his organ. 'Hello, everybody!' Bobby shouted, then strummed loudly on his guitar while Billy started a rock and roll number on his organ.

'They're loud,' said Katie.

Bobby sang:

> *A man with a gun!*
> *A man on the run!*
> *A man with a gun!*

'Is this song about Vince?' asked Franky.

'Shhh,' Lucy answered.

> *We were rockin' and a rollin'*
> *In the supermarket,*
> *When this guy came speeding past us*
> *Like a super-sonic rocket.*

Next door at the Thompsons' house, June, Walter and Caroline were eating TV dinners and watching the show.

'Mom, do you think Lucy is watching this tonight?' Caroline asked.

'I'll bet she is!' Walter laughed.

June shot Walter a stern look and replied, 'I think so, honey. But remember Lucy told us all about Vince. The Silverellis' song doesn't necessarily tell the *real* story.'

'Shhh! I'm trying to hear the words!' Walter complained.

The Silverellis' voices floated out from the Thompsons' big television set:

> *Hey Bud! I sang out,*
> *That's no way to shop,*
> *Slow down those wheels*
> *Or I'll have to call a cop.*

A small well-behaved crowd of teenagers were clustered in the television studio. They had been instructed to look like they were enjoying themselves and to scream, cheer and clap at the appropriate moments. The camera zoomed in to give viewers at home a glimpse of their enjoyment.

Gloria and Bob Jameson were sitting in front of their television, watching the Silverellis sing.

'Aren't they good!' Gloria enthused. 'What do you think, Bob?'

'Hmmph,' Bob answered as the Silverellis sang:

> *My words seemed to bug him,*
> *And this is what he said,*
> *Just give me all your money,*
> *Or you'll wind up dead.*

> *'Cause I'm a man with a gun!*
> *A man on the run!*
> *I'm warning you son,*
> *I'm a man with a gun!*

'Wow, is that what Vince really said?' Katie asked as the Silverellis played their instruments furiously for a few minutes and jumped up and down with some oddly inspired dance moves.

'I don't know. I wasn't there,' Lucy answered, blowing smoke rings at the television.

The Silverellis continued:

> *He emptied the cash register*
> *And headed for the door,*
> *People were just screaming*
> *And diving for the floor.*

'I knew the minute I saw Vince that he was bad news,' June clucked with disapproval.

'You thought he was great,' Walter interrupted. 'I distinctly remember you saying, "He's just great, Lucy! What a nice guy! Keep a hold of him!"'

'That's not true!' June interjected.

'Yes it is,' Walter said, wagging a finger and June pulled her lips into a tight line.

> *Hey, he looks familiar!*
> *Someone yelled out loud,*
> *Well, you'd better forget you saw me,*
> *The thief shouted to the crowd.*
>
> *'Cause I'm a man with a gun!*
> *A man on the run!*
> *A man with a gun!*
> *Yeah, I'm on the run . . .*

Probably the entire population of Tinicum was craning towards a television set. This wasn't just the Silverellis' big night. It was a big night for their town. Come on, boys, thought the population of Tinicum. You can do it. This is your big day – and a big day for us too.

The Silverellis sang out with gusto:

> *Just forget you saw,*
> *That I broke the law,*
> *'Cause I'm on the run,*
> *And I've got a gun.*

The twins danced around some more, while playing some complicated things on the organ and guitar, then Bobby did a final leap and it was over.

'Wow,' Katie remarked. 'I told you old Stink-face was a creep.'

'That's enough,' Lucy said sternly.

'Wow,' Franky enthused. 'Can I learn to play the guitar, Mom?'

'You're too young. Maybe in a few years.'

Ed Sullivan came out and joined the Silverellis on stage. 'And that was the Silverelli Brothers, folks. Great, boys, just great!'

'Thank you, Ed,' they replied.

'Now tell me, boys. I hear that new song of yours, "Man With a Gun" is based on a true story. A story of something that really happened at the Acme supermarket where you work?'

'That's right, Ed,' Bobby answered. 'It was on Friday night a couple of months ago. We always try to liven things up a little by practising our singing at the back of the store. But on this particular Friday, this guy came in, filled up his cart with groceries, then pulled a stocking over his head and ran up to the grocery line. He pushed everyone out of the way and instead of paying, pulled out a gun and told the cashier to give him all the money in the registers. He ran for it and drove off in this red convertible.'

'Is that so?' said Ed.

'Yeah,' enthused Bobby. 'And the thing is, no one had really taken any notice of him until he had run up to the cash register with that stocking over his head. A couple of people thought that the guy seemed familiar, but they just couldn't place him. Later on, a few girls mentioned that a guy called Vince had a red convertible. Word started going around the neighbourhood, but nobody could believe this guy Vince would have done it. He seemed OK, you know? He had a nice girlfriend who had two kids. But by the time the police were told and they drove around to the girlfriend's house, both cars were gone. It looked like the whole family were on the run. But the police found out that the girlfriend had nothing to do with the robbery. She ran off because Vince had threatened her with the gun. And Vince – he just disappeared.'

'That's some story,' Ed said to Bobby.

'Yeah, but a true one. We like to think of it as a modern American folktale. A little bit like the kind of songs that Dylan guy sings. But more modern, you know? We like real American rock and roll music. Elvis is our hero.'

'Well, thanks a lot, boys.'

'No problem, Ed. Any time.' And Bobby and Billy Silverelli walked off the stage to a flurry of hand clapping from the pack of teenagers, which was supplemented by taped cheers and applause supplied by a sound technician.

Backstage, the studio teenagers were lined up waiting quietly for autographs. Bobby started signing the little autograph books then turned to Billy. 'Hey! That was great, wasn't it!'

'Yeah,' Billy shrugged. 'It was fun.'

'*Fun!* It was terrific! Great! Wild! This is it. It's all go from here.'

'Who says?' asked Billy.

'Look,' Bobby said, spreading his hands out towards Billy. 'When you sing on TV, you've hit the big time. Nothing can stop us now.'

Billy just shrugged and put his name in a few more of the little books.

'Well, Jimmy, what did you think of the Silverelli Brothers?' Ed asked Jimmy Claxton at the end of the show. Jimmy was a seasoned talent scout who set up new acts with a few gigs and took a big cut from their pay.

'Well, they're a little old fashioned,' Jimmy drawled while puffing smoke from his cigar. 'Times have changed. Know what I mean? Buddy Holly died ages ago – it's all long hair and British accents now.' Jimmy took a few slugs from his double bourbon, then clamped his cigar back between his teeth. 'I could probably get them a few gigs in Vegas though. Support act for Liverace or something.'

'Liberace,' Ed corrected.

'That ain't his name on the circuit, if you know what I mean,' Jimmy sneered, wagging his cigar at the ashtray. 'But he's always looking for new talent.'

'Good, good,' smiled Ed. 'I'm glad you think they have a future in show business.'

'Yeah,' laughed Jimmy. 'You could say that. Something like that.'

Lonesome out in Space

They had been working on the spaceship for about three months. Time was running out though. Katie and Franky would be going back to school in two weeks.

'Don't worry,' Mrs Weatherby said. 'I'll keep working on it while you're at school and you can give me a hand in the afternoons and on weekends.'

Katie seemed dubious. 'I was hoping that we could try it out before then,' she said.

'I think it still has a long way to go,' Mrs Weatherby smiled.

They had started building the spaceship at the beginning of the summer. It had taken a while to convince Mrs Weatherby that it was a good idea to build one in her garden, but Katie was extremely persistent.

Katie and Franky had met Mrs Weatherby one afternoon while they were on an expedition. Mrs Weatherby's place had always been slightly off limits, and the other kids told stories about Mrs Weatherby being very weird.

'We've heard that she kidnaps kids and hides them in that old house of hers,' they would say. This was enough to interest Katie. 'Let's go exploring,' she said. 'And I know where.'

*   *   *

Mrs Weatherby's place wasn't like anything they had seen before. It was as though a miniature golf course surrounded her house. They wandered around looking at the strange things in her garden. 'This is a map,' Katie said. 'Look – North Dakota.' She pointed at a group of life-sized Indians huddled in a semi-circle. They were like big statues, but decorated with pebbles and bits of glass which gave them colour. A soldier stood nearby, holding a US flag. The Indians looked very sad.

As they walked along, strange creatures peered at them from the trees. 'Wow,' said Katie. 'You never know what you'll find next.'

Then she gave a yelp of surprise and Franky stumbled into her. A lady – not really old and not really young, had stood up right in front of them. 'I thought you were a statue,' Katie said.

'I don't think so,' the lady smiled.

'Is she a witch?' Franky whispered a little too loudly to Katie. She jabbed him in the ribs with her elbow.

'Are you kids lost?' Mrs Weatherby asked.

'Not exactly,' Katie answered.

Mrs Weatherby just looked at them expectantly.

'We're on an expedition.'

Mrs Weatherby laughed and said, 'Well, explore away. If you discover anywhere new, let me know about it, will you?'

Franky and Katie spent most of their summer vacation wandering around Mrs Weatherby's garden. They would help her fix up the place and try out new ideas. Garden probably wasn't the best word for Mrs Weatherby's place. She had more land than anyone for miles around. Mrs Weatherby would make ice-tea and tell them the story behind each place in her garden.

'My husband Hank was a truckdriver,' she explained. 'We practically lived in that truck and went all over the place together. And we had a dog named T-Bone. We would all sit in the front of the truck and sing songs to make the miles go faster. We were all terrible singers, but we didn't care. There's a nice sort of freedom moving down an empty road at sixty miles an hour, the wind blowing through the truck, singing your heart out with no one to turn around and tell you that you're not any Frank Sinatra or Peggy Lee.'

'So where's your husband Hank?' Katie asked.

'Dead,' Mrs Weatherby answered.

'How did he die?' Katie wanted to know.

'In a truck crash.'

'But *how*?' Katie waited for the answer while Mrs Weatherby stared at Katie and Franky for a minute.

'You know,' she finally said, 'it's not always very polite to ask people questions like that. They might get upset.'

'But we don't know anybody who died,' Katie explained. 'All the dead people we know about died before we were born. What's wrong with asking how someone died?'

'You should ask your mother questions like that.'

Katie and Frankie thought about this.

'But what happened to your dog?' Katie finally asked.

Mrs Weatherby was silent for a few seconds. 'He died too. We were all singing – well, T-Bone was barking – and went flying up this hill on a country road in Louisiana when all of a sudden this huge monster of a truck came up over the other side, right in our lane. I can still remember it all like it was in slow motion. Hank tried to spin the wheel and throw us off the road. T-Bone gave a yelp and the windshield burst into thousands of pieces.

'I woke up lying in a field near the side of the road. The local sheriff was standing over me and I heard him say,

"Jesus. She's alive." It was like my head was underwater. I tried to ask questions, but nothing came out right. They wouldn't talk to me. They put me on a stretcher, but I saw how the truck was demolished and Hank was on another stretcher with a sheet over him. The other driver was OK – a big guy who kept wringing his hands and saying, "Will she be all right? What about her?" They checked me over at a hospital in New Orleans and let me out the next day. I never got to say goodbye to Hank though.

'I stayed drunk for ten days straight and don't even remember telling them to cremate Hank and T-Bone and to send the ashes back to Tinicum.'

Katie and Franky were quiet for a few minutes. 'Is that why you moved back to Tinicum and built your garden?' Franky asked.

'I think so,' Mrs Weatherby answered. 'It gives me something to do. All this keeps me company and helps me remember what I've seen and done.'

No one could think of anything to say and they just sat there and finished their ice-teas.

Katie, Franky and Mrs Weatherby talked a lot more after that. She told them stories about all the places she had been to, what Hank and T-Bone had thought about them, and why she had designed a sculpture in a particular way. Franky and Katie told her about the people in the neighbourhood. 'The place sure has changed,' she would shake her head and say. 'When I was a little girl and lived here with my mother and grandparents, you couldn't see anything but cornfields for miles around. The only people we ever met coming or going were truckdrivers.'

'It's the space age,' Franky would tell her. 'Things change fast. Soon no one will need to work and we will be able to have little spaceships instead of cars.'

Katie perked up when she heard this. She said to Franky as they walked home for supper, 'I've got a great idea. If it really is the space age like you said, why don't we build a spaceship? Mrs Weatherby would be good at it. She can build anything.' The idea was launched.

They asked Mrs Weatherby about it the next morning. She just laughed. Every day for an entire week, Katie kept pestering Mrs Weatherby about the spaceship.

'Why do you want to do this so much?' she asked.

'I want to be the first girl astronaut,' Katie answered.

Franky thought about it a minute then said, 'I want to go up into space and see where God lives.'

Mrs Weatherby laughed and said, 'Well, that's as good a reason as any. Yeah, why not. I wouldn't mind seeing the old fella myself some time.'

So they worked together through the summer. The spaceship slowly began to take shape. Katie became more and more excited.

'It's going to take a while,' Mrs Weatherby kept saying. The rocket was looking pretty good from the outside. Katie would climb inside and make Franky yell out the countdown before take off. Katie would make roaring noises from inside the rocket then yell, 'Katie Simon – first girl in space!!'

It was almost September and Katie and Franky didn't have much time left before they had to go back to school.

'Do you think we can try it out soon?' she asked.

Mrs Weatherby was carrying a large bucket of broken glass to decorate the outside of the spaceship with. As she put the bucket down, she made a strange noise and fell forward. The glass spilled from the bucket in a multi-coloured stream. She slipped over and lay in a crumpled heap near the spaceship. Katie and Franky stood looking at her for a few seconds while Katie said quietly, 'Mrs Weatherby – are you OK?'

Franky shook her gently by the shoulder, but she didn't answer.

They both stood there looking at Mrs Weatherby. Something like ice expanded in their chests and they could hear the heaviness of each other's breathing.

'You wait here,' Katie said to Franky.

Katie ran all the way home and got their mother to call the hospital. When the ambulance arrived, two attendants jumped out and went over to Mrs Weatherby. 'Heart attack,' one said to the other. They pushed violently on her chest and Franky waited for Mrs Weatherby to yell with pain, but she just lay there with her eyes closed. They tried a few more times, without success. The attendants shook their heads and put her on a stretcher then into the back of the ambulance. Katie ran back up to Franky just as the ambulance pulled away, light flashing and siren screaming.

Katie and Franky walked home without talking. They could see most of the neighbours standing around their mother, whispering like static. When they saw Katie and Franky, the neighbours came towards them, asking a lot of questions that Franky didn't seem to hear.

Franky looked at these people who seemed to live in a world short on oxygen and long on talk. Their mouths moved, but the volume was turned down. Silent questions kept bumping into him as he watched their mouths pushing at the air, like gasping fish or creatures who had ended up on the wrong planet. They towered above him, making him dizzy.

Franky felt himself floating and the darkness of space rushing in to separate him from everyone else. It was bigger than anything that had touched him before. It was like walking in space without a rope to anchor him.

Leaves of the Sea

Joycie opened the box of photos Mother had sent to her and started sifting through them by date. She had almost five decades spread around her when she found the book bound up with a ribbon lying at the bottom of the box. It was dark green and had water stains mottling the leather cover.

Joycie slipped the ribbon off and opened the book. 'Frederick Stitzenger, 1886'. The handwriting was slightly spidery, but beautiful. It reminded Joycie of frost spread across a window. She flicked over the first page.

Pressed between the leaves of the book was a deep red frond of algae, clinging to the paper with a memory of the sea and the dust of salt. She looked at the lacy thing, almost afraid to turn the page and dislodge it into nothingness.

But it held to the page, and paper after paper revealed another plant from the sea: ochre, deep green, scarlet, plum. They were neatly pressed in place like the finest embroidery.

Words clung to other pages, the ink spread as delicately as the algae fronds. They spelled out the weather, the rolling of the sea, the moon careening from silver to disc to darkness. She looked at small poems written in German and saw how the clumsy phrases of English improved through the pages.

Joycie thought about the small room in the house she grew up in. The small room where her grandfather sat drinking rum and painting strange red designs on things. She remembered how her stomach used to shrink inside every time Pops looked at her. She remembered how much she had hated everything about him. He was old, he was a drunk, he smelled like bad weather and alcohol.

She held the old book and read words which put a skeleton inside the skin of the man she remembered with more hate than love. He had been a romantic young boy from a small village on the North Sea. From the time he could walk he had gone down to the harbour every day to watch the ships and breathe the atmosphere of the place. At fifteen he ran away from home and was given a job helping the cook on a ship bound for Spain. He rarely set foot on land for the next year.

Joycie pieced her way through this time in his life. She watched how the collection of sea-flowers grew thinner towards the middle of the book and anecdotes of strange cities, bars, and the hunting of whales took over. She read about his recollections, his hopes and private dreams that he had never described to anybody else.

She then found picture after picture. Lines tracing the boundaries of mystery, ignoring the sameness of the everyday. Strange women with fish-tails. Ships with huge sails. Birds skimming the waves. A running tiger – she recognized the tattoo on Pops' arm. The words finished and the final few pages were drawings of faces, maybe people he had known.

It was a different world. It sang with the edge of odd harmonies that haunted her at night. She felt something she could remember, but did not want to think about. It was a persistent emptiness, a dark space impossible to fill.

Joycie closed the book and wrapped the ribbon around it. She placed it gently back in the box, as carefully as the body of a stillborn child.

Night Shift

It was Sunday morning. Most of the neighbourhood seemed to be gathered around the Thompsons' mailbox.

Caroline Thompson was a nurse. She knew how to cut herself, but the blood scared even her and she drove into the all-night Sunoco station where she passed out over the steering wheel.

They took her to Abington Hospital, the hospital where she worked as a nurse. They wrapped white bandages around her wrists and pulled long white sheets over her. She lay there, small, barely a footprint in the snowy white.

It wasn't much of a habit. When no one else was looking she would slip tablets, powders, liquids into her bag – any drug she could get her hands on. There was plenty of stuff in the hospital, she reasoned. No one would miss it.

Caroline Thompson had started working at Abington Hospital when she was nineteen. She had worked as a student nurse, scraped through all her exams and qualified as a registered nurse. But a fear nestled deep in Caroline's stomach – she knew that she didn't remember half of what she had managed to put on her test papers and the regularity of her day-to-day routine allowed even more information to slip away. Caroline couldn't stop worrying, couldn't stop thinking about her inadequacy. She had decided to be a nurse with this vague idea of helping people, but soon felt incapable. The gnawing deep in her stomach started up whenever her work routine was disrupted. Emergencies threw her into a panic. Caroline felt with all her heart that she was an imposter. 'Some day,' she would whisper to herself, 'I'll be found out.'

Every day she slipped her white uniform on and secured her watch just over her left breast. She felt her heartbeat speed up to match its persistent, but fragile ticking. The worry would coil up inside Caroline and moisture gathered under her clothes as she gulped down her third cup of coffee before driving to the hospital.

Caroline would pace through each day, white shoes marking recognized patterns along the polished corridors, cigarettes punctuating her breaks. Exhaustion hit her in waves as she drove home, chainsmoking with relief, her nervous fingers staining the paper.

She would collapse in front of the television every night, watching soap operas, game shows, sitcoms, the eleven o'clock news, until the slipping forward of her own head ended with a hard jerk which abruptly brought her awake.

Her mother would say, 'Caroline, just go to bed. There's no point propping those matchsticks under your eyelids.' Caroline would drag herself to bed and June Thompson would sigh and say to her husband, Walter, 'God, they work them hard. You'd think a nice job like that wouldn't run you into the ground.'

A young doctor, observing the continual tremor in Caroline's hand, wrote her a prescription and told her to get it filled and take a long weekend. The tranquillizers helped for a time and Caroline stepped up her prescription by collecting extra vials of the pills from the hospital dispensary whenever a convenient moment occurred. She felt a levelling blanket of calm settle around her and the fear was, somehow, muffled underneath it. She felt she had been given a reprieve.

The nice young doctor, Gerry Stover, kept refilling her prescription, accommodating stronger doses without any questions. One day he quietly asked her if she minded taking a prescription to a patient for him – pay on delivery. She agreed.

Soon Caroline was dropping off prescriptions to quite a few of Gerry's patients. By falsifying prescriptions and diluting stocks of certain drugs, a steady stream of chemicals floated out of the dispensary into Caroline's handbag. She would drive into Philadelphia, then go wait in a bar or a particular bus stop until her contact arrived. Gerry had quite a network of buyers set up – from ex-patients with long-standing habits all the way down to nervous high-school kids trying to act tough. Caroline became his middleman and was given a selection of uppers and downers in exchange for camouflaging Gerry's operation. She began to keep more and more erratic hours, but her parents were glad she was finally establishing some sort of social life.

Caroline did enjoy her 'nights out'. The unpredictability and atmosphere of danger appealed to her at first. She would fortify herself with an extra dose of tranquillizers and wait, half in a dream, for someone to approach her, to press up against her at the bus stop. There was a strange sense of comfort in this desperate intimacy. Something she couldn't find at the hospital.

But someone began to get wind of the raids on the dispensary and rumours began to circulate. Gerry disconnected all contact and Caroline didn't have the access to the dispensary that Gerry had had. Her nerves couldn't stand the strain and she collapsed one day in the canteen. She was ordered to take a holiday – they would discuss her job when she came back.

That Friday night, Caroline went up to the Pocono mountains to stay in her parents' cabin. She drove all night on her nerves and a bottle of No-Doze. As she drove, the tension curled up again like a spring inside her. Her fingers could barely hold her cigarette. She knew she was a failure – it was impossible to go back to the hospital. They would know everything by now. She drove watching the headlights skitter over the road, seeing shadows mix with the morning mist into shapes as terrifying as her nightmares.

She pulled to the side of the road and sat panting, sweat dampening her clothes. Her heart was ticking twice the speed of her watch. She bent over the steering wheel and started crying, unable to stop.

At 5 a.m. Caroline took the pack of razor blades from her handbag. She was a nurse, she knew how to cut herself, but the blood scared even her and she drove into the all-night Sunoco station where she passed out over the steering wheel.

It was Sunday morning. Most of the neighbourhood seemed to be gathered around the Thompsons' mailbox. They talked quietly, trying to figure out where it had all gone so wrong.

Gone at the Root

The sofa was firm enough for long-term TV viewing, but soft enough for a nap during commercials. A coffee table was centred in front of it, wood-sealed with this special kind of polish that stopped damp beer glasses from leaving a mark. You could put your feet up on this coffee table, but Max and Lil never did when company was over.

The men sat at the bar Max had built, drinking beer and criticizing the football game. The women leaned towards each other on the sofa, Bloody Marys doing no damage to the coffee table as they talked about wigs.

'I've always wanted to be a blonde,' admitted Sandra, 'but you know what bleach can do to your hair – breaks it right off. Bill always liked my hair long, so I had to make a choice – stick with the long brown hair, or go blonde but maybe it falls out.' The women laughed and swallowed some of their drinks.

Lil gently patted her curls. 'You know, it was pretty much the same with me and permanent waves. My hair; straight as a yardstick. Ever since I was a kid I'd roll it with this, roll it with that, but the curl would drop right out. Thought about trying a permanent wave, but I was kind of worried that my hair might break off if the waving went wrong.

Max liked my hair long, so I forgot about the waves – stuck to smooth sailing . . . ' Sandra and Lil laughed again.

Max looked at Bill and said, 'Want another beer?'

'You bet.'

The beers snapped open and Max notched up the volume with the remote.

'It's funny how a hairstyle can change you,' reflected Sandra. 'You have this whole different attitude, like you're somebody else.'

'Yeah, like a secret agent or a movie star, or someone without a mortgage.'

'Or an airline stewardess, or the president's wife, or someone with a live-in maid . . . '

The women laughed, then Lil held her empty glass towards Max. 'Hey, bartender, we're getting a little dry over here.'

Max frowned and said quietly, 'You two know you're not supposed to be drinking.'

'C'mon now, it's a holiday! How many New Year's Eves do you get in a lifetime? Another drink for me and my friend here.' Lil put her arm around Sandra.

'Yeah, Max, who wants to ring in the New Year dry? You've got to honour tradition,' Sandra admonished.

'Yeah,' Lil agreed. 'A little drinking, a little dancing.'

Sandra started to sing, 'Let old acquaintance be forgot—'

'That's not right, is it?' Lil interrupted.

'Don't know, never understood that song,' shrugged Sandra. 'C'mon, boys, let's have a toast.'

Max and Bill looked at each other. Max silently handed the women two more drinks. 'Here's to old friends and new hairstyles,' Lil began.

'Here's to old memories and good times,' Sandra added.

They all clinked glasses and had a long drink. 'Here's to doctor's orders!' Lil drained her glass. Sandra did the same.

Lil got up and made two more Bloody Marys. Max didn't say a word.

'Here's to another year,' said Sandra. They all tilted their glasses back at the same time. Sandra was quiet for a minute, then asked Lil, 'You got any more of those pills?'

'A couple, sure. Your head hurting?'

'It's from the drinking. You know the doctor told you not to drink, Sandra.' Bill was getting agitated.

'C'mon, Bill. It's New Year's Eve.'

'Here's to nineteen seventy-nine, the end of a decade,' Lil chipped in. 'And a new start in the New Year.'

'You've got to break the rules sometimes,' Sandra continued. 'Have a little fun. Remember driving to the country and drinking that farmyard beer when we were kids?'

'Yeah.' Bill carefully made patterns in the condensation on his glass.

'Well, here's to Prohibition.' Sandra swallowed the codeine tablets Lil gave her, then emptied her glass. There wasn't much more to say, so they sat and watched the television until it went midnight. Bill and Sandra walked home in the first few minutes of the New Year.

Later that night, when Lil was snoring gently, Max slid out of bed and padded into the bathroom. Three wigs decorated styrofoam heads without faces. The hair felt funny, like a doll's. Max opened his shaving bag and took out a small box. He pulled out the long lock of hair, tied neatly in the middle, and stroked it. He had secretly taken it when the hair first started coming out in clumps in Lil's brush. He could never joke about the wigs like Lil and Sandra did; in fact, he pretended there weren't any wigs at all – that everything was normal.

Max looked in the mirror, examining the bags under his

eyes, the lines on his forehead, his defeated chin, while those heads of hair, faceless, expressing neither hope nor fear, watched him for a very long time.

Screen Doors

For a while she thought she was going crazy. People would hand her change in the bar and their touch would make her feel dizzy. If Lucy went shopping, strangers bumping against her while waiting in line would make her feel strange. She would lean slightly their way, feeling how their bodies moved gently against hers like boats moored too closely together in a harbour.

Sometimes Lucy would inadvertently catch the eyes of a man she didn't know and he would smile at her. This worried Lucy, but she couldn't stop whatever it was that she was doing.

One night at work, a stranger started flirting with her. Lucy joked around with him a little. He was kind of nice looking and his attentions made her feel pretty good. The guy's name was Jay and he was still hanging around near the end of the night.

'Hey, Bud,' Hal said abruptly. 'It's closing time. Ready to clear out yet?' Lucy was surprised. She'd never heard Hal speak to a customer that way before. Jay looked at the two of them, shrugged, and left.

Hal kept rubbing already-dry glasses with a cloth. Lucy thought he looked different. She noticed his eyes were a sea-green, not blue like she had thought. The muscles in his arms moved as he worked on the counter, eyes focused on an imaginary smudge. Lucy watched him from the corner of her eye and thought about what he had said to Jay. And thought about why. She found herself re-interpreting small things that Hal had said or done in the past and she was surprised at how she felt. She couldn't remember the movement of time from just looking at Hal to kissing him full on the mouth.

Their kisses moved them clear across the bar and into Hal's apartment at the back. Lucy felt a little drunk and disconnected from her body, but strangely awake at the same time. She was partly floating while watching every-thing from a distance. Buttons opened under her fingers and cloth moved away as she slipped her hands through the hair on Hal's chest. She wanted to touch the entire land-scape of him and trace his contours with her hands, her skin, her tongue.

Sometimes they were almost silent, their breath and salt mixing as they found the best ways to move together. And sometimes this quiet man spoke to her, asking her questions she had never heard before, telling her to do things she had only thought of secretly. Lucy found herself whispering in ways that amazed her – someone else's thoughts seeping from her mouth like the sweetness of violets or the tang of blood. It was like listening to another language and sud-denly finding that you understood.

Almost from a distance Lucy watched their bodies slip over, under, and through each other. Her breasts moved across his chest and she tasted the pools of salt gathering in the hollows of his neck and rolling down his belly. He would follow the lines of her, retrace her features, place small kisses along the stretch marks that circled her stomach.

In the flickering shadows of that night, she could see the angles of her skin moving with a special geometry. A type of perfection she hadn't noticed before. She was exposed; pale skin like the belly of a fish glinting white and silver, twisting in the boundaries of another element. But she felt no fear, only the need to be nowhere else but there, to possess and to be possessed completely. There was nothing but that room, that darkness, that air heavy with the mixture of their bodies.

They made love most of the night and as the light began to change, Lucy curled up within Hal's arms and lay half asleep, breathing his scent like a faraway place.

Lucy drove home at dawn and sat smoking in the living room until it was time to pick up the kids.

Hal and Lucy never let on that anything had changed at work. They joshed each other and exchanged small talk the same as before. Sometimes Lucy couldn't resist looking at Hal, checking his reaction to things. She would look up and find that his eyes were already on her.

But no one who came into Ed's guessed that anything had changed. Lucy and Hal would slide past each other behind the bar, not quite touching. The hairs on the back of Lucy's neck would prickle, but her face would show nothing.

Their nights together were like a summer full of August. The heat gave substance to the air, which was rolled and shifted by the darkness. They seemed to fit together perfectly and never tired of each other. Hal would sometimes ask Lucy out to dinner or to the movies, but she always said no. He didn't press her on it, too afraid to destroy what was perfect in itself. An unspoken feeling pulled them together.

When they were in that one room, the rest of the world

ceased to exist. The familiar was always replaced by the need to discover something new. After making love, they would stretch out next to each other on the bed and she would fit her toes into the arch of his foot. She would press her ear to his heartbeat and just listen as they waited for the sunlight to gather under the curtains.

Lucy wanted nothing else. What she had was enough – two kids, her friends, the house, a car, her job. She didn't want to be anywhere else. And she didn't want another person in that little world she had struggled to pull together.

Lucy never let Hal come to her house. She wanted their worlds to be separate and felt a collision between the two would throw her out of orbit. She was afraid that one lie or every-day deception would make her crash and shatter into a million pieces, or that she would fall like a meteor spinning down from space and scorching the earth with fire too hot to breathe.

Every morning that they woke up together was the same. Lucy would get dressed and gather her things. Hal would follow her to the screen door. There was always a moment of awkwardness, padded by the kind of silence grown inside a church. Hal would look at her quietly, then would kiss her gently through the mesh after she shut the screen door between them.

Cowboys

Franky dragged the overalls on top of his jeans and T-shirt, pushed his feet into his boots and laced them up. He heard the removal van honk outside and ran out the front door. 'See you later, Mom!' he yelled. The door slammed before he heard Lucy's reply.

'You ready, kid?' Bud Sawyer said from the window of the van.

'Yeah,' Franky answered.

'Right. Meet you over at the house, then.' Bud roared off and Franky could hear furniture slide and bump around the back of the van. Franky was helping out Bud during the summer, trying to save up some money so he could pay for his first year of music college. Rusty had said that he would pay for both Katie's and Franky's college education, but Franky knew that Rusty would have been happier if Franky had been studying architecture and Katie had taken up music. So Franky was determined to pay his own way and not feel obliged to listen to any of Rusty's advice. The removal business paid pretty well and Franky was pleased to see that shifting furniture was pumping up his muscles as well as his wallet.

Franky reached the Lovells' old place just as Bud was

trying to back the van up the drive. 'How am I doing with that mailbox?' he asked.

'Coast looks clear,' Franky answered. 'Back her up.'

Bud and Franky walked inside the front door. Joe Potter was already there, moving some bags of rubbish that had been left behind. 'Hi, guys,' he said. 'How much stuff do the new people have?'

'A full van,' Bud answered. 'And not all the breakables are marked, so take it easy. Any cracked plates come out of your salary.'

'You've got to be kidding!' Joe laughed. 'I heard you gun that van over the kerb. If there's a plate left in one piece, I'll be surprised. And I'll testify against you to Mrs Cutter,' he threatened.

'God, you wouldn't,' Bud said with mock terror. 'Well, come on boys, let's get a move on it. She's driving over here in an hour and a half. Let's enjoy the peace and quiet while we can. And Franky, put those two six packs in that old fridge before they get warm.'

'Yes, sir,' Franky saluted with his beer.

Franky strolled down the hall towards the kitchen. Although he had never been inside the place when the Lovells had lived there, he could still remember his way around. He smiled as he remembered the time he and Katie had broken a window and sneaked inside when the place was in between owners. Katie had been caught, but nobody had told Lucy. Or if they had, she had never done anything about it. Come to think of it, Franky mused, it would have been just Lucy's kind of thing. It would have made her laugh.

Franky remembered Katie climbing up on to the window-sill of the picture window, her gun poised . . . the smash of glass. His fear.

Franky looked around him. It's so empty, he thought.

196

He could find few clues that the Lovells had ever lived there.

I wonder if they left anything at all, Franky thought. He put the beers in the fridge, then decided to have a quick look around before helping Joe and Bud with the furniture. Franky felt a little like a spy, or maybe some kind of pervert. He had always had a big crush on Pam Lovell and half felt that he might find some secret left behind by mistake. 'I'm just checking out upstairs for any junk to throw away,' Franky yelled. 'I'll be down in a few minutes.'

Franky went down the hall and looked in the bathroom. He opened drawers and the medicine cabinet, feeling like a thief. Nothing. Greg Lovell had been pretty thorough in his evacuation of the place. Most people left stuff behind. Enough puzzle pieces to put together some kind of image of them.

He found the room that used to belong to Pam. He remembered the evenings – two long summers full of them, when he used to look up at that window and watch Pam walking back and forth, half hoping to see something more than her silhouette, half hoping not to. There wasn't much left. Marks where some posters had been. Dust. Some pretty floral paper on the walls. Some hangers in the empty closet.

Franky thought of Pam. She was the most beautiful girl he had ever seen and, of course, she had never really noticed him. Sure, she said hello and all that stuff, but she was too busy flirting with the football captain to notice a nobody like him. To notice a skinny, would-be musician, with a spattering of acne.

Pam had been in the year ahead of him and a year behind Katie. She was one of the prettiest girls in the school – tall, thin and very photogenic. Pam was determined to be a model and spent all the money she earned working weekends at the dress shop down at the mall on photographs for her portfolio.

It had been something of a scandal when the Lovells moved into the neighbourhood. Greg Lovell was a handsome lawyer who worked down in Philadelphia. He had two teenage daughters, but no wife. Clarisse had died ten years before and although he dated a number of women, he had not remarried. Greg joined the country club and was an excellent golf and tennis player. He had a quick wit and was always the first to offer to buy a round of drinks. 'He's a pretty good guy,' the men in the neighbourhood would say. 'But he just doesn't quite fit in.'

'He's a nice man,' the women would say. 'Imagine raising those girls all by himself. It's surprising that a good looking man like that – and a lawyer too – hasn't found himself another wife.'

'Probably would have if he hadn't left Philadelphia,' someone would say.

'This is a family neighbourhood,' someone else would add. 'It's tough to meet single people.'

But no one invited him to join the neighbourhood gourmet club where five different couples took turns having each other round for special meals. Greg Lovell was a great cook. They all knew that from the time he had invited all the neighbours around for a big barbecue. And they were all impressed with his house; reproductions of paintings by famous artists hung on the wall in expensive frames. His wife had collected special antiques, glassware and silver bric-à-brac bought in Europe, which complemented the dark, expensive-looking furniture. Pictures of Greg's wife were everywhere; in silver frames on little tables and bookshelves. A large portrait of her hung over the fireplace. Lori, the youngest daughter, looked just like her – with her pale, toffee-coloured skin and large green eyes. His wife had modelled in Paris and mutual friends had introduced them at a cocktail party in New York City. She had died in a car accident when she was twenty-nine.

Greg felt like someone had left him for dead – heart beating, but body feeling nothing. He spent hours cataloguing the sins of his life, trying to work out the cause for such a punishment. Greg had had so much success in his life, his wife's death felt like a special warning from God not to get too cocky. He worried that everything he had struggled for would collapse all at once and he would be left alone and confused like a vagrant in his old neighbourhood. If it wasn't for the two girls, Greg probably would have taken his car and driven off the same bridge with the flimsy guard rail into the river. But instead he hired a nanny and sent the girls to a private school.

When Pam was ready to start junior high school, Greg decided to sell their apartment in Philadelphia and move out to the suburbs. He had heard too many stories of kids with drug problems at the expensive school he had sent the girls to. He wondered if their school was that much better than the tough high school he had gone to before getting a scholarship to Columbia – more for his football skills than for the high grades he had worked so hard to earn.

Greg hadn't counted on the impact he would make on Tinicum when he moved in. A black man with two light-skinned daughters, no wife and a better job than any of the others in the neighbourhood.

But his fear of pride instigating another tragedy gave him incredible patience and he worked hard to become part of the place so that his daughters would feel they belonged. The girls had less trouble fitting in than their father, even though there were still only five other black kids in the entire high school. The local boys thought Pam and Lori looked exotic, maybe French or Italian, like foreign movie stars. They had no shortage of admirers. Pam was home-coming queen during her senior year at high school, a testament to how well she fit in.

Greg started to worry about whether he had made a mis-take and was inadvertently encouraging his daughters to pass for white – just as Clarisse's mother had in the early fifties. He had the girls apply to all-black colleges and invited black friends with eligible sons to their house for supper.

But Pam went off to study fashion design in New York City, a year after Katie had gone to New York University to study architecture. Katie ran into Pam every once in a while at a bar they both liked in the Village. Pam always waved and said hello, then would glide off to be with her trend-setting friends.

Lori moved up to New York City too. She followed in her father's footsteps and went to Columbia to study law. After both girls left home, Greg Lovell sold the house, left Tinicum and moved back to Philadelphia.

Franky could hear Bud yelling for him. 'Hey, Franky! Are you going to give us a hand or what!'

'I'm coming!' he shouted down the stairs.

He looked around the room once more. It felt so empty. Not exactly defeated, but more like some big promises had been broken. It felt exactly the same as it had the day they sneaked inside. Franky and Katie had looked everywhere with big expectations for some kind of treasure, but found nothing but yards and yards of empty space.

Driving to Minneapolis

'Daddy, I forbid you to drive! Joe and I bought you and Mother airline tickets!'

'I don't like flying. You better try and get your money back.'

'Be reasonable. You're seventy-one years old. I don't think you should be driving all the way to Minneapolis.'

'I don't care what you think. I've been making up my own mind for almost seventy-one years and I'm not stopping now because my daughter has decided to do all my thinking for me.'

Max hung up the phone and walked over to the refrigerator. He pulled out a beer, opened it, had a long drink. He walked into the living room where Lil was lying on the sofa, watching the ball game.

'Hey, beautiful, who's winning?'

'Who do you think? The Phillies. Give me a sip of that stuff . . . '

Max frowned, but handed her the can. 'You all ready to take off for Shangrila tomorrow?'

'Shangrila, hah. Next best thing to a nursing home. How did we end up with such a bossy daughter?'

'Takes after you, that's how.'

Lil snorted with derision just as the door swung open and a voice yelled, 'Anybody home?' Lucy walked in, carrying a pizza box. Franky ambled awkwardly after her, smiling his gawky smile and carrying a couple of cans of coke and a six pack of Bud.

'Hiya, sweetheart! Hey, Franky! You're early.'

'Yeah, I thought we could have some dinner before I have to go to work. You like pepperoni, don't you?'

'You bet,' Lil said.

'Whoa, careful partner!' Max laughed as Franky's beer frothed out of the can and fizzed on to a cardboard box near the sofa. 'You'll ruin the furniture.'

They all sat together, watching TV. There was an odd sense of quiet in the house. Not just the sort of quiet that accumulates in empty rooms and echoes between the wall and ceiling. But the sort of quiet made up of words too awkward to be said.

'Well,' Lucy announced at last. 'Guess I'm going to have to go to work, and Franky has a hot date tonight.'

'Ahh, Mom!' Franky started to object but Lucy cut him off. 'We'll stop in tomorrow before you take off.'

'Hey, hon, you have any of those funny cigarettes?' Lil asked. 'They stop my head from hurting so much. Might be good for the ride.'

Lucy laughed and handed her a Marlboro pack. 'I rolled some for you, but be careful where you smoke them – you know they're not legal.'

'No one's going to arrest an old woman dying of cancer, are they?'

'I wouldn't bet on it,' Lucy said.

The phone rang at Ed's bar. 'It's for you Lucy!' Hal yelled down the bar.

Joycie's voice ran through the receiver. 'Lucy, can't you

make them see sense? They can pick up the tickets at the airport. Just drive them there.' Despite the miles between them, Lucy could hear Joycie drumming her fingers on the kitchen counter.

'I think Daddy's made up his mind, Joycie.'

'Well, make him change it,' Joycie snapped.

'If you couldn't change it, why should I be able to?'

'You could at least try. Do you really think Mother will last a three-day journey? And you know how bad his driving is at the moment. He just doesn't pay attention. He'll cause an accident.'

'It means a lot to them, Joycie.'

'Well, it's damned irresponsible. How are you going to feel if they cause an accident and kill somebody?'

Lucy sighed. 'OK, I'll try. Talk to you tomorrow.' She hung up the phone, went back to the bar and made herself a double vodka and coke.

It was 10 a.m. when Franky zoomed Lucy's old Mustang up the drive. 'Jesus!' Lucy complained, hauling herself out of the car. 'You drive just like your father used to.'

'He always says you were the crazy driver.'

'Yeah, what does he know,' she smiled. Lucy rang the doorbell like it was the jingle to some song, then opened the front door and walked inside.

'Hey, sweetheart, how was work?'

'Same as usual . . . pretty good I guess. You guys all set to take off?'

'Just about,' answered Lil.

'Here, give me that.' Lucy took a big box full of food from Lil. 'I'll put it on the back seat, OK?'

Soon the car was full. Suitcases were strapped to the top and the doors just about closed. They stood in a semi-circle near the car, a hush of reverence hanging over the driveway.

'Well,' Max announced. 'I guess it's time to go.'

Nobody could think of much to say.

'Well, then,' said Max. 'Give us a hug goodbye, kids.'

Franky hugged Lil first, his 6 foot 2 inches dwarfing her frailness. Then he and Max embraced and thumped each other on the back. Lucy kept hugging everybody and saying, 'Drive carefully. Give me a call every night and as soon as you get there.'

'It's a long ride,' Franky said.

'Yeah,' replied Lil. 'But we're used to it, sweetheart. We've done a lot of travelling in our time and this is just a drop in the bucket, believe me. If you talk to Katie before we get there, give her our love.'

'I will. Well, have a good drive,' Lucy said a little helplessly. 'Don't forget to call.'

Max carefully adjusted the rear view mirror, then sprayed the windshield for the third time. 'Do you think we're crazy, Lil?'

'Why would I think that?'

'It's a long ride.' Max stared at the double yellow lines as the car wove hypnotically along the edge of them.

'We've done longer.'

'I don't drive as well as I used to,' said Max.

'You have to take some risks in life. Otherwise, what's the point?' Lil shrugged. They kept driving down the turnpike, a steady 45 miles an hour, while cars in a big hurry zoomed past them, yelling advice.

'I'm getting a little nervous,' Lil whispered.

'Don't worry, hon. It's only going to take us a couple more days. We'll be OK.'

'I mean . . . we promised we'd never do this, Max.'

'I know, Lil,' he said softly.

'Not after having your father live with us for all that time.'

'This will be different. Don't worry.'

'How do you know it will be different?' Lil asked a little sharply.

'Because there's two of us. We can take on Joycie together.' Max turned his head to smile at Lil.

'It won't be the two of us for ever.' She turned to look out the window.

Max started watching the lines on the road again. 'Let's just enjoy our freedom while we can,' he said quietly.

Lil watched the scenery flick past. They were finally out of Pittsburgh and the green and trees were looking just like Erwinna.

'This looks kind of like home, don't you think?'

'Pretty much,' answered Max. 'But I get this feeling that Minneapolis is going to be real different. It's going to be an exciting place to go to.'

'Oh is it now!' Lil laughed.

'Yeah,' Max continued. '*Real* exciting. So exciting you won't know whether you're coming or going. So exciting you won't have time to watch TV, there will be that much to do.'

'Like what?' Lil questioned with a smirk.

'Like what? What do you mean, *Like what?* Minneapolis is a hubbub of activity. Minneapolis is the centre of the world. I've been told by reliable sources.'

'Oh, yeah?' Lil grinned.

'Yeah. Just wait and see. It'll be all go.'

'You always were an optimistic man,' Lil chuckled.

'I'm going to be sick, Max.'

'In the tupperware, just throw up in the tupperware. I'll find a gas station. Don't worry, hon.'

Lil dipped her head over the plastic bowl and weakly spat into it. Max concentrated on the road. He was amazed how straight the double yellow lines were.

How do they paint these lines, he wondered.

'You want to play some cards?'

'Cards? When I'm driving?'

'Things will be much better in the countryside.'

'What do you mean, Lil?'

'No bad influences. No hoodlums.'

'Like who?'

'Like that crazy neighbour – that pervert across the street.'

'Fred? What's wrong with Fred?'

'Always wearing that stupid fishing hat. And that beat-up Chevy in the drive – a disgrace. Bad influence . . . '

'What do you mean?'

'Every night, with the curtains wide open and the light on, he stands in the living room and takes his trousers off and walks around in his skivvies.'

'What?'

'Yeah. The kids told me.'

'What kids?' Max asked.

'*Our* kids. They stand and watch. He makes a big production . . . slowly takes the trousers off and then sits down to watch TV – skinny old legs poking out of white boxer shorts. Drinks beer and eats potato chips with nothing on but an old T-shirt and boxer shorts. With the curtains open.'

'I don't know what you're talking about, Lil.'

'It won't be like that out in the countryside, away from all these bad influences. We have to think about the kids, Max.'

Max was confused. 'But we've thought about the kids all our lives, Lil.'

'But sitting in boxers with the curtains wide open is perverted. Hanging them on the washing line is one thing, but when someone's wearing them, that's another story. Who wants to see that? They won't do that in the country, I'll bet.'

Max looked at Lil for a while and almost swerved off the road. She was talking more to herself than to Max and he couldn't make much sense out of what she was saying. He watched her out of the corner of his eye. His hands gripped the wheel nervously.

'So are you getting ready for Joycie's? We're almost half-way there now.'

'What?' Lil looked at him like he was crazy. 'I'll never be ready for Joycie's. You know I don't want to leave Erwinna. We worked hard for years to get that place. I still think we should have stayed – Joycie is supposed to be our daughter, not our babysitter.'

'C'mon, Lil, you know she's only trying to help. Would you rather have a daughter that didn't give two beans for what happened to us?'

'Yeah, well, OK,' Lil mumbled. 'But you know, I'm not one for accepting favours.'

'Sometimes though you just have to back down a little bit.'

'Joycie has to learn that too.'

'Before she's sixty-eight years old.' Max looked at Lil and raised his eyebrows.

'Sixty-eight,' explained Lil with dignity, 'sixty-eight is the prime of life. Take it from a woman who knows. It's when you're sure what's real and what isn't.'

'I could get used to this.' Lil was turned towards her window, watching the cigarette smoke curl out of the gap at the top. 'There's something quieting about just watching the scenery go past. So much to look at, changing almost too fast to really take it all in. Never knowing what's coming up next.'

Max turned to her and smiled. 'Yeah,' he answered. 'I know what you mean.'

'Can't we just keep going?' Lil asked. 'Just keep driving until we reach California and see the Pacific rushing up against the beach. Why don't we just do that? We've never driven all the way to California. It's a once-in-a-lifetime chance.'

Max looked at Lil. 'That's thinking big,' he said. 'That's a long trip. I don't know whether I've got it in me.'

'Sure you do, kid. Sure you do.' Lil smiled at him, then leaned over and flicked on the radio.

They kept on driving mile after mile, not saying much, just humming along to the music. They kept driving until midnight, just so they could watch the flickering neon of the next city spell out some stories all around them.

Sleep is Contagious

The man behind her sneezed loudly twice. She imagined microscopic droplets floating her way. Katie knew she would have a cold in a day or two. She had taken the wrong seat, again. In a coach full of disgruntled old people. Two particularly garrulous oldsters sat behind her. They never stopped talking, mixing complaint with observation, with demand. The young attendant was at her wits' end. Her tone had become sarcastic, but they didn't notice. The train was full, so Katie had no hope of finding another seat.

Miles of cornfield, miles of woods, a few condensed miles of skyscrapers and crumbling tenements. Katie looked out the window. She was amazed at the amount of space without people. Houses were isolated into small communities, almost feudal city-states linked to the outside world by only a few roads, the railway, the radio and maybe a TV. Even mass media couldn't change these places much. Ways of doing things had been handed down from generation to generation – a blueprint for living.

They had travelled through the Rockies hours ago and the sprawl leading to Denver had started. Katie looked at words spreading messages. 'Pressed Steel Pulleys and Stampings.' A wall had a collection of 'I loves' sprayed on it. 'Alonzi's Pizza.' A brick façade of a building spelled out: 'Chuck's Hard are S ore.' Letters go missing, words take on new meaning. Small houses with backyards tugging at the railway tracks tried to make an impression with their lawn ornaments.

A voice came over the speaker, cheery, overly expressive. Something like the voice of a presenter on a TV game show. There must have been a staff contest on, to see who could annoy passengers the most. Kill 'em with kindness. 'Denver coming up,' the voice informed them. 'Will all that are detraining make sure that they have all of their possessions. Denver next stop.'

The man got on at Denver. 'Is this seat free?' he asked.

'Yes,' Katie assured him.

'Mind if I sit here?'

'No, go ahead,' Katie answered.

He arranged himself, then his duffle bag near his feet. Katie's heart sank. She had been lucky so far. She'd had two seats to herself since Anchorage. Katie managed a couple of hours' sleep each night and shifted her crumpled limbs from one position to another, then slept for another hour or so. Tonight would be difficult.

They pulled out of Denver. Katie heard the man behind her complaining again, his voice like gravel. 'Look at that over there,' he said to his wife. 'Those phones in the parking lot are all smashed up. You know, when you talk about phone booths, that's another sign of the times. You can't put anything out that some vandals ain't going to tear down.'

'You're sure right,' his wife agreed. 'That's the truth. What do you think of that, young lady?' she asked the attendant. The attendant pushed past their seat and didn't say a word.

The man next to Katie turned to her. I hope he isn't

going to start talking about phone booths too, she thought.

'Do you want a coffee or something?' he asked. 'I'm just going to get myself a coffee from the dining car.'

Katie smiled. 'No thank you,' she said.

Katie settled back in her seat. They passed through an expanse of woodland. She thought about the vastness of Alaska and wondered how New York City would seem to her now. She had just spent the summer before her final year at college in Alaska working in an architect's office. They tried to design buildings that would blend into the landscape – not something that most people who lived in Alaska seemed to worry about. Her classes would be starting up again in two weeks and she was going to spend a few days at home with Lucy and Franky before heading back to college.

New York City and Anchorage. Some things about the two places were similar: the overpowering sense of the skyscrapers and the miles of pine trees leaning down from the mountains; the drunks on Fourth Avenue; the peepshows; the look of defeat on faces in the rougher parts of downtown Anchorage. There was a feeling of danger in both places – guns or rifles, knives, a need for big money. Alaska left you feeling slightly delirious: adrenaline was set rushing by the surprise of big animals crossing your path, the thought of unpredictable grizzlies, and so much overwhelming space. It still had the feeling of the dream about it – big money from oil, new land to claim, and a new start. People always joked that being an Alaskan was like being on the run – from your past, your lover, or yourself. Katie could believe that. In New York City there was a sense of big dreams that had been knocked over and chipped around the edges. Or shattered into smithereens.

The man arrived back at his seat. 'I drank my coffee in the dining car,' he explained. 'I got talking to a fellah in there and thought I'd better drink my coffee before it got cold. I sure hope you didn't want anything.'

'No, not just now,' Katie smiled.

The gentle rolling hills changed to flat cornfields. Katie wondered what State she was in. Grass was cut in huge swishes by a tractor. The town was small. Houses huddled together in long, crouched rows. They were painted pastel shades and were surprisingly pretty. The sunlight glinted on farm equipment. Roads spread out like octopus tentacles. Katie wondered who lived in those houses and what they did.

They pulled into a small station in a town called Gailsburg. Suddenly Katie was sitting in someone's backyard, watching while they toasted marshmallows. She was almost embarrassed. Just the glass of her window separated her from their summer evening.

The train headed under a canopy of huge blue-black storm clouds. The little white house in the distant field glowed in the strange light. Stacks of hay were scattered across the landscape. Sun poured in the left side of the train while clouds boiled on the right. Lightning spilled into the open field and Katie felt exposed. The emptiness frightened her. The rain sliced down the train window. The old woman behind her said, 'It's raining now.'

A dirt road near the train track was already a muddy stream. An irrigation pump sprayed a field, doubly baptized in the rain. She wondered how the settlers felt. The vast space, the flatness, the isolation.

The man turned, looked at her from the gap between the top of his glasses and the brim of his ball cap. 'I have to say, I wanted to sit next to you. Because you're skinny. I was real scared I'd end up next to somebody fat, and wouldn't be able to sleep.' That thought had certainly crossed Katie's mind, particularly when she watched a number of very large women squeeze down the corridor between the seats.

'Yes sir,' he continued. 'A big fat lady sat down next to me on the bus once. I tried to stick it out, but I could barely breathe. I finally had to get up and say to her, "I don't mean to be rude, but there isn't room here for both of us." I went and sat down next to a skinny fellah.' Katie smiled while he laughed and slapped his knee. His eyes were magnified behind his thick lenses. He looked like some kind of woodland creature with his big eyes, fawn-coloured clothes and skittish manner. 'I'm sorry, I shouldn't interrupt your reading. But I do like to talk. I'll try and be real quiet while you read.'

The train steward walked past carrying a tray full of food towards first class. 'Man with a baby!' he called out. 'Coming through – man with a little baby.' He laughed as he wobbled and walked. The smell of the food made Katie hungry and she pulled out some sandwiches.

Another cheerful voice came over the loudspeaker. 'We're approaching the Mississippi,' it announced. 'If you look out the window while we cross the bridge, you'll be able to see the back of the train coming around the bend.'

A large swampy area preceded the Mississippi. The river was huge and the town crept down to it. People here will all have boats in their yards, Katie thought. The rain had swept through and cleansed the place. Aqua-blue trucks and cars filled a parking lot. The buildings all had art deco shapes, and the store fronts were straight out of an Edward Hopper painting.

Every once in a while the man next to her turned and told her something about himself. He was on his way home from visiting his daughter in Cold Springs, Colorado. She married an Airforce man. He wasn't all that impressed with Cold Springs, but it was good to see his grandkids every once in a while. Colorado was pretty good for fishing too, he thought. But he still preferred Pittsburgh. 'Pittsburgh is my home town,' he explained. 'And you kind of get used to a place when you've lived there all your life.'

By 10 p.m. it was too difficult to read by the dim lights left on in the car. People were lying under blankets, sprawled in unlikely positions for sleep. The man opened his duffle bag and pulled out a sleeping bag. 'Here,' he offered, unzipping the bag into a large quilt. 'It gets cold here at night.' He spread the cover over her knees.

Katie told him not to worry – she had her coat to put over her. But he insisted. 'This is plenty big enough – see, it stretches across both seats.'

The carriage was asleep. Coughs, snores, restless limbs disturbed the grey light. Katie drifted in and out of sleep, her head leaning on the window edge, buffered by a small pillow and her coat. Her lapses into sleep became fewer as the man next to her took over more and more of the seat each time he shifted position. Katie wished there was an arm rest between them. She pressed herself further against the window, but his back was still huddled up to her side. She soon found it impossible to even doze, and searched outside for any glimmer of light. She was afraid that if she stood up, she would lose her seat for good and would have to wake him and half the carriage in her efforts to get it back.

Katie finally got up at six and went to sit in the dressing lounge for an hour. When she returned to her seat, he was awake and asked her where she had been. 'I woke up and you were gone,' he said with surprise. 'Did you sleep all right? Every time I woke up, you seemed to be asleep, but you kept pushing the blanket off. I had to keep covering you up.' Katie smiled weakly.

'You know,' he said. 'I just started travelling by train

about five years ago. My wife and I always used to drive everywhere, but she died ten years ago and it took me a while to realize that travelling by train on my own would be cheaper than driving on my own.'

Katie smiled at him sympathetically and he kept talking. 'My wife – she was a perfect woman. Don't get me wrong, we had our fights. Mostly me doing the fighting.' He laughed. 'But she was the sweetest thing. I did think about remarrying and I would have done it if I'd met a woman half as nice.' He paused with a smile and Katie couldn't think of anything to say back.

'I went with one woman for a while – a widow,' he told Katie. 'But you know, and I don't mean to offend you now, but when it came to sex . . . well, she wouldn't.' He whispered the last half of the sentence. '*And* she was a widow. She would just say to me, "That's for marriage."' He looked at Katie, letting his palms rise and drop. 'I told her that I thought she was being a little unreasonable, as she was a widow and all. But she just said to me, "I don't give a *s-h-i-t*."' He spelled out the word in a stage whisper. 'Now my wife never said a curse word. *Never*. And she *hated* that word in particular. I just grabbed my coat and walked out the door. I never saw her again.' He shook his head, remembering that terrible evening. 'OK, sure, she sent me a letter, apologizing and things, but I wouldn't have it.'

He shook his head again and Katie looked sympathetic. 'You know,' he said, 'last night was the first night I'd slept with a woman in ten years. Now I don't want to offend you, but that's what it was like. Curled up under the same blanket with you lying right next to me. I had almost forgotten what it was like to sleep with someone. I liked it,' he told her. 'I'd do it again.' Katie kept a thin smile on her face and inched slightly towards the window.

Katie wondered if he was a little bit like those men she

saw walking into triple x porno theatres near Times Square. The loneliness was often naked and brutal on their faces and dripped from the worn out seams of their clothes.

She was curious and slightly repelled. He watched her with eyes magnified and bright behind the glisten of his lenses. She was distant and somewhat separate from her skin. She felt slightly soiled. Do prostitutes ever feel this way? she wondered.

'Don't worry,' he reassured her. 'We haven't done anything wrong. It's just like we've slept in the same bed, but we haven't done anything. But it was nice.' The attendant came up to get him for detraining.

'Goodbye,' he said, and shook her hand. 'It was a pleasure.'

Five and Dime Dreams

George had just asked his wife Brenda to turn up the volume on the television set when it happened. She lifted up the remote control, pointed it at the TV and suddenly there was this explosion. The space shuttle burst into flames before their very eyes, and Brenda was so frightened she dropped the remote control. The picture fizzled away, and there were a few moments of shocked silence before Martha picked it up and flicked the TV back on.

It was a disaster. People were crying and screaming. There were flames, and the newscaster didn't know what was happening.

George Gardner sat there helplessly, wishing there was something he could do. Guess everybody else must be feeling pretty much the same way, he thought.

'My God!' cried Brenda. 'Those poor astronauts must be burning up. What a tragedy.'

'Now will they go to Heaven instead of outer space?' Martha asked.

'Yes,' George answered, picturing the six men and one woman in big white suits and helmets, weightless and lifeless sliding through Heaven.

'Daddy,' Martha asked, 'will the astronauts send back pictures of Heaven on TV?'

'I don't think so,' he answered.

They watched as emergency teams tried to stop the fire.

The newscaster spoke with emotion tripping up his voice. 'A tragedy,' he said. 'A terrible tragedy – like the Hindenburg disaster so many years ago. We can only wonder what impact it will have on the space programme – on history . . .' His voice trailed away, lost while he thought about the future.

There were special news bulletins for the rest of the evening. The Gardners watched quietly as they learned everything from the television little by little. Pictures of the astronauts were shown on the screen. Reporters told them about the schoolteacher who would have been the first American woman in space. She had trained for seven years to be an astronaut, only to have her family watch the shuttle explode into flames on TV. The Gardners hadn't known any of the astronauts, but they felt like someone from their own family had just died. Something terrible had happened for everyone to see. A big dream had just blown up.

The event left its mark on the neighbourhood for days. People talked about it whenever they met; working in their yards, at the supermarket, playing golf. George noticed that the space shuttle disaster seemed to start up conversation between people who had never spoken much before. But then again, the talk didn't really go all that far either. 'Hello, George,' his neighbours would say. 'Guess you saw it all on the news, eh?'

'Yes,' George would answer. 'A real tragedy. It's like the end of a big dream.'

'Yes,' some would agree, shaking their heads with regret before saying, 'Goodbye, George. See you around.'

Or others would answer, 'Yeah, George, it looks like the

future isn't coming as fast as we thought. Doesn't look like anyone will be selling any houses on Mars for a long time!' They would chuckle a little, then wave before getting back to whatever they were up to. The disaster captured everyone's imagination for a week or so, but they soon slipped back into their routines. George was a little disappointed by this, but not really very surprised. Even something as big as the space shuttle disaster wasn't going to change Tinicum.

The space age had made the world a small place, but in some ways the neighbourhood hadn't changed much over the years. Most people still kept their distance from George and his family, even though they had lived in Tinicum since 1954. George had spent most of his working life as the real-estate agent in Tinicum – right up until he retired in 1981. In fact, he had sold most of his neighbours their homes. But George still didn't really feel part of the neighbourhood. No one invited George and Brenda to their parties or even around for a couple of beers. Maybe they thought the Gardners didn't like to do all the things they did because the Gardners had two grown-up children who still lived at home.

When the Gardners ran into their neighbours, most of them would smile and say, 'Guess you're glad you've retired. The real-estate business isn't so good these days, is it?'

George had to agree that houses in Tinicum didn't seem to be selling as fast as they used to. His neighbours would just shake their heads and say that it was a shame. Tinicum was such a nice neighbourhood, but maybe the houses were a little small and the yards not big enough. They explained that they were thinking of moving further out into the country themselves. A bigger place, a little more land. Somewhere nice for the kids to play.

If Martha or Cindy were with George, people passing always said hello a little too loudly, like the girls were hard of hearing. The neighbours always looked uncomfortable, but the girls never seemed to mind and waved goodbye enthusiastically as they left.

Some of their neighbours hardly spoke to George or Brenda. June Thompson just hurried past with barely a nod. Brenda believed that June blamed the bad luck the Thompsons were having on the neighbourhood. June seemed to hold George personally responsible because he had sold them their house. The Thompsons had been trying to sell their place for quite a few months, but no one wanted to buy it. June and Walter thought that the neighbours told people about their daughter Caroline, who'd tried to commit suicide, and that their place brought bad luck. But the real problem was that those houses weren't that easy to sell just then. It was as simple as that.

Some of their other neighbours still remembered the rumour that Georgie was having an affair with Gloria Jameson. Gloria used to be real nice to Georgie. She gave him a little work raking the leaves in their yard. Georgie didn't do a very good job, but Gloria used to give him fifty cents all the same and fix him lunch. Georgie was about sixteen at the time and a strong boy. He still had a pretty bad temper on him, but he loved Gloria. He would go sit on her doorstep every morning. Gloria felt kind of sorry for him. She would give him odd jobs to do around the house, maybe cleaning a few things. Or she would just let him watch TV. She knew he was lonely. It didn't bother her when Georgie kissed her on the hand and told her she was pretty.

But the neighbours started gossiping, especially as Gloria didn't have the best reputation in Tinicum. People said she went down to the Satellite Lounge to pick up strange men. It was June Thompson who first told the Gardners that everyone was gossiping about Georgie and Gloria.

'Walter and I have probably lived here longer than anyone in the neighbourhood,' she said. 'And we thought we ought to tell you. The neighbours are a little worried about the amount of time your son spends in Gloria Jameson's house.' George was a little surprised and he guessed it showed.

'There are rumours, you know, that Gloria Jameson spends a lot of time at the Satellite Lounge – and it's not with Bob Jameson. She gets drunk every Saturday night and dances with a lot of travelling salesmen.'

George didn't really know what to do. He didn't really believe that Gloria would get up to anything with Georgie. She just seemed lonely like him, and if they were both happy, what was the problem? But Bob Jameson got pretty fed up with Georgie hanging around and one morning screamed at him. The yells scared Georgie, who hit out at Bob, making him fall from the concrete steps on to the front lawn. Bob always had a bit of back trouble, but the fall really did him in and he ended up in hospital. Georgie stayed pretty riled up after that incident and started hitting out at people for no reason. In the end, the Gardners couldn't cope any more. The doctor suggested that they put Georgie in a home for the mentally handicapped. George and Brenda didn't want to do it, but it seemed like the only way, and the best thing for everyone.

Gloria Jameson, Myrna Pepperidge and Lucy Simon were the only neighbours who had ever really talked to the Gardners. Gloria was the only one who ever dropped by their house. She and Brenda had lunch together sometimes – every once in a while George came home and Brenda was all giggly from a couple of Martinis. Gloria seemed to drink a little too much of late. She used to be a good looking woman, but years of living with a man who didn't love her left their mark. Gloria never gave up hoping that Bob would change and things would be the way they were when they first got married. Gloria was a little like Brenda in that way, an optimist. George sometimes thought that kind of optimism didn't always do you much good. The Jameson kids, Tommy and Charlotte, had families of their own now, but they lived in some other part of the country and rarely got back to see Gloria. She and Bob stayed together for reasons that were hard to understand. It wasn't like George really believed in divorce. Couples should try to work things out. Sometimes divorce seemed like the only answer. George didn't think the way Bob and Gloria lived together was too healthy.

Myrna Pepperidge was another story completely. She used to stop Brenda and George in the supermarket and ask after Martha and Cindy. She would insist that the girls enrol in her ballet class and tried year after year to get them to move gracefully through a simple routine. Year after year Mrs Pepperidge was doomed to failure, but Martha and Cindy became a kind of mission with her. She was determined that she would teach them the basics of ballet, and despite her prickly manner the girls loved her. Months after she died Martha and Cindy used to walk over to Pepperidge Pond and feed the ducks, hoping that Mrs Pepperidge would come back.

Lucy Simon had been the Gardners' neighbour for over twenty-five years. She had always been friendly, but George and Brenda had really only got to know her in the last year or two. If they were out mowing the lawn at the same time or sitting in the yard, Lucy would yell over the fence, 'Hey, do you want to have a beer and play some cards?' Sometimes

Brenda and George walked over with the girls and did just that. It was always a little awkward though, because they seemed to be from different worlds. Lucy told George and Brenda stories about the people that came into the bar where she worked, but all of their conversations were like strangers swapping stories. Brenda and George liked Lucy and so did the other neighbours. But she didn't really seem to completely fit in. She was friendly with everybody in the neighbourhood, but there was something different about her. After she and Rusty divorced, she never got married again. People thought it was kind of strange, but Lucy seemed happy enough.

Brenda asked Lucy about it once when they were all playing cards, and Lucy just laughed and said, 'You know what they say, lucky at cards, unlucky in love.' Lucy may have had a point there – she always seemed to win at cards.

'Oh come on,' Brenda said. 'That's just an old super-stition.'

'Well,' Lucy laughed. 'Maybe. Have you ever seen that old James Dean movie, *Rebel Without a Cause*? Well, maybe that's me. Or maybe that's how I always saw myself. Who knows any more? I've never done things the easy way, and it used to worry me. But you know, I don't really care what anyone thinks these days.'

Brenda and George just nodded and smiled. They both knew exactly what she meant.

But it was hard for George and Brenda. Being seventy years old and still having two daughters to take care of. They knew that Martha and Cindy would have to go into a home like Georgie – probably in a year or two. It wouldn't be fair on the girls otherwise. Brenda didn't like to talk about it and she still cried for hours after they came back from visiting Georgie.

Gloria sometimes asked George and Brenda how they

managed. 'Most people expect to look after their kids for around eighteen years, then to have some time on their own. When they hit seventy their kids start thinking about looking after them. You've been raising children for almost thirty years. That's a long time. I just don't know how you do it.'

'The time has just disappeared,' Brenda told her. 'It doesn't seem like anywhere near thirty years. Things don't seem to have changed much in our life. I like that.'

But George knew that things had changed somehow. It was a subtle thing, but the atmosphere was different. Their life had never been easy. George didn't hit the big time when he was a young man. Sure, he was lucky to get the job as a real-estate agent and a nice house outside the city. But luck always seemed to turn a little bit against them. They had done all right though. Couldn't complain.

George had this feeling that everything was a puzzle. But half the time the most important pieces seemed to get lost somewhere under the sofa. You're down there on your hands and knees, George thought, beaming the flashlight underneath, but you still can't find them. Those pieces seem to just disappear, and even if you spend your whole life looking or trying to fill in the gaps with some parts you've made up yourself, it won't really matter. You're still going to wind up with a jigsaw that only shows part of the picture.

Living Nowhere in Particular

The sound of gravel hitting the underside of the car made Charlie snap his eyes open. He twisted the wheel left and got the car back on to the road. He was breathing hard and gripped the steering wheel with both hands.

From the corner of his eye, Charlie could see the houses lining the side of Tinicum Pike. They seemed to be rushing in the opposite direction, hypnotically, in one long straight line. He could almost feel them moving.

Row after row of houses – small, compact, neat. Dream houses with little front yards decorated with special lawn ornaments: men in sombreros riding donkeys; space-age metallic globes; pink flamingoes. An ideal neighbourhood designed by men who promised a future full of spaceships, but delivered tiny stars trapped inside cheap kaleidoscopes from the five and dime.

Charlie had looked at these houses every evening for twenty years while driving to Ed's Bar for a couple of quick drinks after work. There was some kind of comfort in the conformity of their shape and size. Charlie lived in a similar house a few miles down the road in a place called Tinicum. Tinicum was an old Indian name: Algonquin maybe, or Tamenend or Unami.

*   *   *

It was about 7 p.m. on a Friday in late May 1992 when Charlie turned into the gravel drive of Ed's. Friday night was poker night. He waved as the Sylvesters walked past his car, wobbling side by side in perfect harmony and screaming at each other, hearing aids turned down to zero. They smiled and waved back at him, then started their yelling again.

Charlie walked into the bar and went up to the counter. Hal, the owner, was drying glasses.

'Hiya, Hal,' he said. 'Where's Ed?'

Hal just laughed and pulled him some Budweiser. 'You tell me. You've got all the answers.'

Lucy Simon walked into the bar. 'Hey, Charlie!' she called out. Lucy flicked on the neon sign above the counter that spelled out 'Ed's' and Hal poured himself a beer. Lucy took over the drying and made sure everything was just right behind the bar. She was a chainsmoker and a little out of shape, but buxom enough to be the local sex symbol. Lucy knew her stuff though. Name any drink and she could put it together according to the book. She plunked down two beers on a table in the corner for the Sylvesters and readied the 'poker table' with a couple of bowls of potato chips and a big old bottle of Cutty Sark.

Bells jangled as the door swung open, and the rest of the regulars walked into the bar, talking loud and laughing. 'Hey, Lucy!' they yelled. 'Are you ready for the game?'

'You bet,' she said.

'Bet, ha!' laughed Charlie. 'Not any more than I have to with you around.'

'Don't worry – I brought a new deck.' Sammy waved a pack of cards.

Lucy just smiled and poured everyone a shot of Cutty Sark.

'Well, you know what they say,' said Marge. 'Lucky at cards, unlucky in love.'

'Jeez, Marge! That's a rotten thing to say!' Lydia peered over her cards reproachfully.

'Well, I can't deny it,' shrugged Lucy. 'I've been on a losing streak in that department longer than I want to remember.'

'Haven't we all.' Marge fanned her cards and frowned.

Charlie concentrated on his cards. Not much of a hand. Normally he joined in with the banter, telling everybody funny stories about what happened at the plant during the week. But Charlie couldn't drag any more good stories out of his memory that week. He had too much on his mind.

So he stared hard at the cards, a fan full of symbols spelling out different degrees of luck. Hearts, diamonds, clubs, spades – love, wealth, good fortune, death . . . Gambling could take on mystical proportions. Cards had hidden meanings used to predict the future. If he could only control them, will his cards into winning combinations, lucky sequences, special parings, Charlie was certain that his life would follow suit. Gambling and fate, you can't separate them, he thought as he placed the Jack of Diamonds next to the Jack of Spades.

A few minutes later Lucy showed her hand and they all pushed some money her way.

'Christ,' Sammy complained. 'I think you've got a marked deck there. I've never seen anyone win so much.'

Cards were snatched up, thrown down. Lydia tut-tutted every time she picked up a card. 'It's uncanny,' Lydia chipped in. 'If I didn't know you, I'd think you were cheating.'

'I'd say playing with a marked deck was cheating,' Sammy joked.

'You brought the cards, remember?' Lucy replied.

'OK, my deal,' Marge announced, pulling the cards into a neat pile. She shuffled quickly and expertly while Lucy poured everyone another shot of Cutty Sark.

Lydia looked pleased with her hand and groaned when Hal interrupted the game.

'Hey, Lucy,' he yelled. 'The phone's for you.'

Lucy started walking to the back of the bar to pick up the phone.

'Hey, hurry back!' Lydia sang out. Charlie topped up all the glasses again and grabbed some pretzels.

'Lucy?'

'Yeah?'

'It's Rusty.'

'Hi, Rusty, what's up?'

'I've been thinking about you a lot recently.'

Lucy stands listening, not too sure what to say. Rusty sounds a little drunk – slurring his words a bit.

'And I thought I'd call while I had the nerve. Because I was thinking, right, that maybe we should give things another go.'

'What do you mean?' Lucy asked, confused.

'You know, like, get married again.'

'Married?'

'Yeah. It would be better this time. We'd have some money. You wouldn't have to work so hard. The kids would like it.'

'Yeah, well, Rusty – I don't know what to say. I mean, it's been twenty-five years since we got divorced.'

'Well, neither of us got married again, did we? Just think about it, OK? It's lonely in this place. I've always missed you. I've got nothing to do when I'm not working.'

'Must be the life, Rusty.' Lucy blew a smoke ring, but didn't know what else to say.

'Hey, come on, Lucy.'

'Sorry, I wasn't trying to be sarcastic. You have to admit, this is a pretty strange phonecall. I just don't know what to say.'

'Say you'll think about it. You could move down to Florida. All this good weather, you know? Or I'll move back to Tinicum if you really want. We could get married in a church or something.'

'I don't know, Rusty.'

'Think about it, OK? I'll call you in a couple of days, all right?'

'OK.'

Lucy walked back to the game.

'Who was that, Lucy?' Charlie laughed over his drink. 'The internal revenue checking up on your illicit earnings?'

'No, my ex-husband.'

'Oh, yeah?' Marge raised her eyebrows. 'What's he after – money?'

'He seems to have all the money he needs,' Lucy muttered.

'What more could a girl ask for?' Lydia asked.

'Money isn't everything,' Sammy said, shaking a finger. 'Take it from a man who knows.'

'You got something else to offer?' Marge laughed.

'Touché.' Charlie and Marge clinked glasses.

'So, what's the deal? You going to leave us and marry the guy again?' Charlie started dealing everyone a new hand.

'Ha,' said Lucy.

Charlie prayed with each card he slapped down on the table. It was four weeks now since he'd been given his notice. The plant had to cut down on workers and it might even close down altogether. Evidently they could manufacture electronic parts for telephones faster and cheaper in Japan. Less workers meant less foremen and after thirty-five years of working his way up . . . he was out.

Today had been Charlie's last day. He hadn't found the courage to tell his wife yet. Over the last month he hoped they would change their minds. But the reprieve he'd kept praying for never materialized.

He had applied for other jobs, but no luck so far. At his age, fifty-five, it wasn't going to be easy to land something else. This was something that Charlie had never dreamed about. Whenever he thought about the fact that he wouldn't be walking around those concrete floors any more, would never have lunch in the canteen again, would never see most of the guys he had worked with for so many years, his head just started to spin.

And the money. They hadn't managed to save much over the years. If he didn't find a job pretty quick, their savings would just melt away. Then he would end up like those people he had read about – house, car, furniture repossessed. Living on welfare. He looked at his cards in desperation. If he could just win a few games, it would be like a sign. Some kind of sign that things would eventually turn out all right.

Lucy was pretty shaken up by the phonecall and knocked back a few drinks to steady her nerves. She thought about the time she and the kids drove all the way to Florida to see Rusty. On the run from Vince. She could just about picture it. They were wearing matching 'Hushpuppy Hotel T-shirts' and plaid bermuda shorts, like some kind of crazy baseball team. Lucy had a map stretched across her knees and darted a look at it every once in a while. She had a lousy sense of direction and just stuck to the route to Fort Lauderdale that Rusty had marked out for her in red. Vince used to joke about the map and Lucy's sense of direction whenever they got in her car. 'He should have just tattooed it down your arm,' Vince would say. 'Then you'd never have to look at that map again. He should have just done that if he's such a good tattoo artist.'

Vince was impressed that Rusty had made so much money with his tattoo parlour. He had a few tattoos himself and would have thought Rusty was a pretty good guy if it weren't for the fact that Rusty used to be married to Lucy. Vince had a real mean streak to him and it became even nastier when he was feeling jealous. Once, Rusty had driven up all the way to Tinicum on his motorbike to see the kids and Vince had prowled around the bedroom, thumping a wall every once in a while. When Lucy had asked him what the matter was he had whirled around and shouted, 'If he tries anything, I'll know exactly where to find him. That map is all up here now,' he scowled, tapping himself on the head.

'I just can't believe anyone can win so much,' Lydia complained. 'Do you *ever* lose, Lucy?'

'Not that much,' Lucy confessed.

Charlie let his hand fall to the table and poured himself a big slosh of Cutty Sark. 'One game,' he pleaded smiling. 'Can't you just let me win one game? It would be good luck or something. It would make me believe I had a little bit of luck too.'

Lucy just laughed.

'Yeah,' said Marge. 'I keep pushing all my tips across the table to you. All those hours of being nice to people at the diner. Being nice to people you'd love to drop an entire greasy breakfast on. For what? To hand my tips over to you.'

'C'mon guys,' Lucy said. 'I provide the booze and snacks. And it's not like we're playing for high stakes.'

'I don't know about that,' Charlie disagreed. 'Playing for luck is pretty high stakes. Sometimes it's worth more than money.'

Charlie tried to imagine how Vera was going to take his news. Vera had never worked – not even part time. Charlie had been very proud of that. His mother had worked all her life; in a sweatshop in Philadelphia, and then cleaning houses for the rich people in Chestnut Hill. Charlie was very proud that his wife didn't need to bring any money into the household. Charlie was scared, but tried not to let on. He kept laughing and joking and knocking back the Cutty Sark with a beer chaser. He kept willing aces to materialize into his hands, but it never happened. Somehow they kept finding their way into Lucy's. The money kept sliding across the table to Lucy, and Charlie felt every ounce of luck in the room sparkle around her fingers and make all the right cards slip straight into her hands.

Lucy didn't notice that Charlie was acting a little bit strange. Not really laughing or talking too much. She kept thinking about Rusty's phonecall. She kept thinking about the last time she saw Rusty.

The long, tense drive all the way to Fort Lauderdale with the jittery feeling that Vince was right on her shoulder. Then the main drag of Fort Lauderdale. College students hanging around the bars, trying to look casual in skimpy swimsuits, desperate to get the best possible sun tan in the last few weeks of summer.

The place was bright, an assortment of colours and signs shouting in the late summer sun, trying to sell big promises. Then there it was, Rusty's place, bigger than Lucy remembered it. A neon sign flashed persistently in the sunlight. 'Tattoos and Motorcycles' it spelled out in red, blue, yellow and green. Lucy parked the car and woke up the kids. 'We're here,' she announced.

'Yay, Daddy!' they yelled.

The shop was smothered in pictures, examples of what Rusty could do. A young girl was sitting in the middle of the room, having a parrot tattooed on her left shoulder. 'Have a seat,' shouted Rusty without looking up.

The kids sat, suddenly feeling shy. 'Mommy,' asked Katie. 'Can I pick out a tattoo?'

Rusty looked up and almost dropped the inking needle.

Later, they were sitting in Rusty's house behind the shop, Lucy and Rusty on opposite ends of the sofa and the kids sandwiched in between. The only other piece of furniture was a giant colour television set.

Rusty looked embarrassed and said, 'The place needs some fixing up. Maybe I should buy a coffee table. You know me, Lucy, I never was any good with decorating and stuff. I've got money, but I don't know what to do with it except buy another bike, and I've got four already.'

'Do your tattoos cost that much?' asked Lucy.

'Not really. I have the only tattoo parlour in town. Zoning laws. I set up my place before the locals decided tattoo parlours would bring down property values. I got to stay, but no one else was allowed to set up shop. I kind of have a corner on the market. College kids really go for them. But I am good, Lucy. They say I'm one of the best.' Rusty looked down at his hands, embarrassed.

'I know that,' said Lucy.

They sat quietly for a minute or so. 'Listen, Rusty. Could you take care of the kids for a while. I'm in a little trouble.'

'What kind of trouble?'

She paused for a minute, not very sure what to say. 'Well, remember Vince? You met him when you came to visit the kids.'

'Yeah.' Rusty didn't look too happy thinking about Vince.

'Well, he has this bad temper and he gets a little mean

when he's drunk – and I think he may have a gun . . . '
Lucy gave Rusty a brief run down, her stomach twisting up
with the irony of it all. She tried to smile. 'I guess we're on
the run and need to lie low for a while.'

'Just stay here, Lucy. No strings attached.'

Lucy thought about it for a minute and said, 'OK. Just
until Katie has to go to school.'

The two weeks disappeared quickly and Lucy realized
that she was getting too accustomed to the long hot days
and dinners out in a different Fort Lauderdale restaurant
every night. In most places, they seemed to get drinks on
the house.

'Just look at this,' the cook or the bartender or the waitress would say. 'Rusty did this beauty.' Then they would
roll up their sleeve or flick up a skirt to reveal a small
masterpiece of a tattoo.

But it was almost twenty-five years later and lot of water
had gone under the bridge.

As Charlie shuffled the cards, he thought about a song his
father used to sing during the Depression. He sang it to
himself as he dealt the cards:

> *I went into a beanery*
> *To get a bite to eat,*
> *I was hungry clean down*
> *From my head to my feet.*

> *So I picked up a doughnut*
> *And I wiped off the grease*
> *And I handed the lady*
> *A five-cent piece.*

> *Well, she looked at the nickel*
> *And she looked at me,*

And she said, 'Kind sir, can't you plainly see?
There's a hole in the nickel,
There's a hole right through . . .'
Said I, 'There's a hole in the doughnut, too.'

He looked at his hand – nothing special. That's been the story of my life, Charlie thought. Not a great hand, but enough to get by on. It's a thin line, between the beanery song and working your shift like normal at the factory. But one day, the cards go all wrong or the rug's pulled out from under your feet. Next thing you know, you're checking the lining in your coat for small change.

Charlie remembered the day he and Vera moved into their house in Tinicum. It was brand, spanking new just like all the things they were going to put inside it. Wedding presents mostly: pots, pans, sheets, towels, dishes and enough booze to stock the bar in their basement. They had bought their furniture – an olive green suite with little rust-coloured throw cushions – on hire-purchase. They wallpapered the living room and bedroom themselves. The living room had boomerang shapes with little squiggles like atoms in rust and olive green. Vera said it was very fashionable. The bedroom was pale yellow and aqua 'with shapes inspired by Miro,' Vera said. Vera took evening classes 'to broaden her mind'. She had learned about modern art and French cooking the winter before their wedding. Charlie was very proud of Vera. They had a house decorated with flair, their neighbours always said, but it was still a house comfortable enough to relax in. And Vera made all of her own clothes. She's a fine woman, Charlie thought. He wondered if she would leave him for someone with more to offer – like a job. He tilted a big gulp of whiskey down his throat.

They kept up the game until about 4 a.m. Lucy had

smoked four packs rather than her usual two, using her cigarette as an excuse for not talking much.

'Well, I'd better hit the road,' announced Marge. 'The diner opens in an hour and I can't keep my truckers waiting.'

'I've got the grandkids for the weekend,' Lydia explained. 'Sharon's rich, married boyfriend is taking her somewhere expensive for a few days. I don't know what I'm going to do with that girl,' she sighed.

'The rich part is OK,' Marge drawled around her cigarette. 'She just needs to delete the married bit.'

'Bring her along to the next game,' Sammy suggested. 'I'm up for grabs.'

'I'm not sure you're her type,' Lydia frowned.

'Hey!' Sammy held out his palms towards them all. 'Am I a catch or what? C'mon, guys, back me up here!'

They all just laughed, shoved back their chairs and got ready to leave. 'Bye, Lucy!' they all yelled. 'See you next Friday.'

Hundreds of tattoos. Lucy could just about see them. Some were pictures from Florida: palm trees, bright birds, alligators. And others memories of Rusty's past: anchors, ships, ELVIS in big letters. The heart on his arm tattooed with her name . . . Memories had a way of coming back to shake you up.

Lucy tidied up the bar and thought about the phonecall that evening. She remembered driving back home from Fort Lauderdale. Rusty followed behind them on his motorcycle for about five miles, pressing on his horn and waving like he was part of a presidential cavalcade or something. She wondered about living in Florida. She thought about her friends at Ed's Bar. And Vince – he never turned up again. Who can understand how people change when they live with each other? If the kids were still *kids*, would that make any difference? Too many questions, too many demands. She remembered all those places scattered on both sides of the red line on the map connecting Tinicum with Fort Lauderdale. She needed some sleep. Lucy walked towards the back of the bar to Hal's apartment. It doesn't matter where you are, she thought.

Charlie drove down Tinicum Pike, his car making patterns across the line down the middle of the road. He managed to pull into the neighbourhood safely and watched the light spread over Tinicum. The cars gleamed in their driveways. The grass was patterned into neat green squares marking boundaries. The houses looked the same, but their doors were painted different colours.

In the early morning everything was too clear. Charlie sat in the car for a while, forehead on the steering wheel. He could feel the neighbourhood around him. He wondered how much longer he would be able to live in this place he knew so well.

He watched the early morning shadows shift and thought about the fear. The fear of having everything that you've dreamed of taken away. Just like that. Snap – like turning off the TV. It's a big fear, he thought, nothing to laugh at. It slaps you in the face in the morning, you hear its murmurs in the afternoon, you feel its breath at your throat in the evening, it sends black dreams to hunt you down at night.

Sadness washed over him, swishing like a curtain, making a sound he could almost hear. Tinicum waited outside his car. He looked at the perfect houses, the lawns and mailboxes. The neighbourhood all done up too neatly; a small-town whore dressed up in her maiden aunt's skirt, blouse and cameo for church. Charlie could almost hear its nervous breathing in the crisp, cheerful morning light. 'Please don't,' it whispered like a prayer. 'Don't,' it pleaded. Tinicum sat there, hardly daring to breathe in fear that someone would look too closely and uncover the deception.

Morning . . .

But the nightmare won't stop coming . . .

As Lucy nears the top of the hill she can suddenly see it two cars back, the red convertible glinting in the sun, tailgating the car in front of it. She thumps the accelerator as the convertible pulls out to pass.

She pulls out too, but the car in front of her refuses to let her pass. She takes the corner too wide, swerving, gravel flying. She looks in the mirror, sees the red fender nosing forward, and fear clutches at the inside of her stomach. Her fingers try to grip the steering wheel, but slide in the moisture from her hands.

In one big slow arc, a piece of gravel swoops like a meteorite and sends her wing mirror into a blistering shower. Its glinting pieces clatter on the windshield, bright like diamonds from Heaven. Each contains the face of a man she can just about recognize as he smiles behind the wheel of his red convertible.

Out of the blue...

INDIGO

the best in modern writing

FICTION

Nick Hornby *High Fidelity*	£5.99	0 575 40018 8
Kurt Vonnegut *The Sirens of Titan*	£5.99	0 575 40023 4
Joan Aiken *Mansfield Revisited*	£5.99	0 575 40024 2
Daniel Keyes *Flowers for Algernon*	£5.99	0 575 40020 x
Joe R. Lansdale *Mucho Mojo*	£5.99	0 575 40001 3
Stephen Amidon *The Primitive*	£5.99	0 575 40017 x
Julian Rathbone *Intimacy*	£5.99	0 575 40019 6
Janet Burroway *Cutting Stone*	£6.99	0 575 40021 8

NON-FICTION

Gary Paulsen *Winterdance*	£5.99	0 575 40008 0
Robert K. Massie *Nicholas and Alexandra*	£7.99	0 575 40006 4
Hank Wangford *Lost Cowboys*	£6.99	0 575 40003 x
Biruté M. F. Galdikas *Reflections of Eden*	£7.99	0 575 40002 1
Stuart Nicholson *Billie Holiday*	£7.99	0 575 40016 1
Giles Whittell *Extreme Continental*	£6.99	0 575 40007 2

*IN*DIGO books are available from all good bookshops or from:

> Cassell C.S.
> Book Service By Post
> PC Box 29, Douglas I-O-M
> IM99 1BQ
> telephone: 01624 675137, fax: 01624 670923

While every effort is made to keep prices steady, it is sometimes necessary to increase prices at short notice. Cassell plc reserves the right to show on covers and charge new retail prices which may differ from those advertised in the text or elsewhere.